A Midsummer Night's Dream

William Shakespeare

SADDLEBACK
EDUCATIONAL PUBLISHING

Saddleback's *Illustrated Classics*™

SADDLEBACK
EDUCATIONAL PUBLISHING
www.sdlback.com

ISBN-13: 978-1-56254-922-0
ISBN-10: 1-56254-922-7
eBook: 978-1-60291-160-4

Printed in Guangzhou, China
0511/05-02-11

15 14 13 12 11   5 6 7 8 9

Welcome to
Saddleback's *Illustrated Classics*™

We are proud to welcome you to Saddleback's *Illustrated Classics*™. Saddleback's *Illustrated Classics*™ was designed specifically for the classroom to introduce readers to many of the great classics in literature. Each text, written and adapted by teachers and researchers, has been edited using the Dale-Chall vocabulary system. In addition, much time and effort has been spent to ensure that these high-interest stories retain all of the excitement, intrigue, and adventure of the original books.

With these graphically *Illustrated Classics*™, you learn what happens in the story in a number of different ways. One way is by reading the words a character says. Another way is by looking at the drawings of the character. The artist can tell you what kind of person a character is and what he or she is thinking or feeling.

This series will help you to develop confidence and a sense of accomplishment as you finish each novel. The stories in Saddleback's *Illustrated Classics*™ are fun to read. And remember, fun motivates!

Overview

Everyone deserves to read the best literature our language has to offer. Saddleback's *Illustrated Classics*™ was designed to acquaint readers with the most famous stories from the world's greatest authors, while teaching essential skills. You will learn how to:

- Establish a purpose for reading
- Activate prior knowledge
- Evaluate your reading
- Listen to the language as it is written
- Extend literary and language appreciation through discussion and writing activities.

Reading is one of the most important skills you will ever learn. It provides the key to all kinds of information. By reading the *Illustrated Classics*™, you will develop confidence and the self-satisfaction that comes from accomplishment—a solid foundation for any reader.

Step-By-Step

The following is a simple guide to using and enjoying each of your *Illustrated Classics*™. To maximize your use of the learning activities provided, we suggest that you follow these steps:

1. ***Listen!*** We suggest that you listen to the read-along. (At this time, please ignore the beeps.) You will enjoy this wonderfully dramatized presentation.

2. ***Post-reading Activities.*** You have successfully read the story and listened to the audio presentation. Now answer the multiple-choice questions and other activities in the Study Guide.

Remember,

"Today's readers are tomorrow's leaders."

William Shakespeare

William Shakespeare was baptized on April 26, 1564, in Stratford-on-Avon, England, the third child of John Shakespeare, a well-to-do merchant, and Mary Arden, his wife. Young William probably attended the Stratford grammar school, where he learned English, Greek, and Latin. Historians aren't sure of the exact date of Shakespeare's birth.

In 1582, Shakespeare married Anne Hathaway. By 1583, the couple had a daughter, Susanna, and two years later the twins, Hamnet and Judith. Somewhere between 1585 and 1592, Shakespeare went to London, where he became first an actor and then a playwright. His acting company, *The King's Men*, appeared most often in the *Globe* theatre, a part of which Shakespeare himself owned.

In all, Shakespeare is believed to have written thirty-seven plays, several nondramatic poems, and a number of sonnets. Quoted often, Shakespeare's lines and characters are immortal. In *A Midsummer Night's Dream*, Puck says, "Lord, what fools these mortals be!" Those words have been echoed by actors for centuries.

In 1611, when he left the active life of the theatre, he returned to Stratford and became a country gentleman, living a quiet life. Then, on April 23, 1616, William Shakespeare died and was buried in Trinity Church in Stratford. Shakespeare is considered one of the greatest writers of the English-speaking world.

William Shakespeare

A Midsummer Night's Dream

Puck

Theseus

Lysander

Demetrius

Bottom

Helena

Hermia

Oberon

Titania

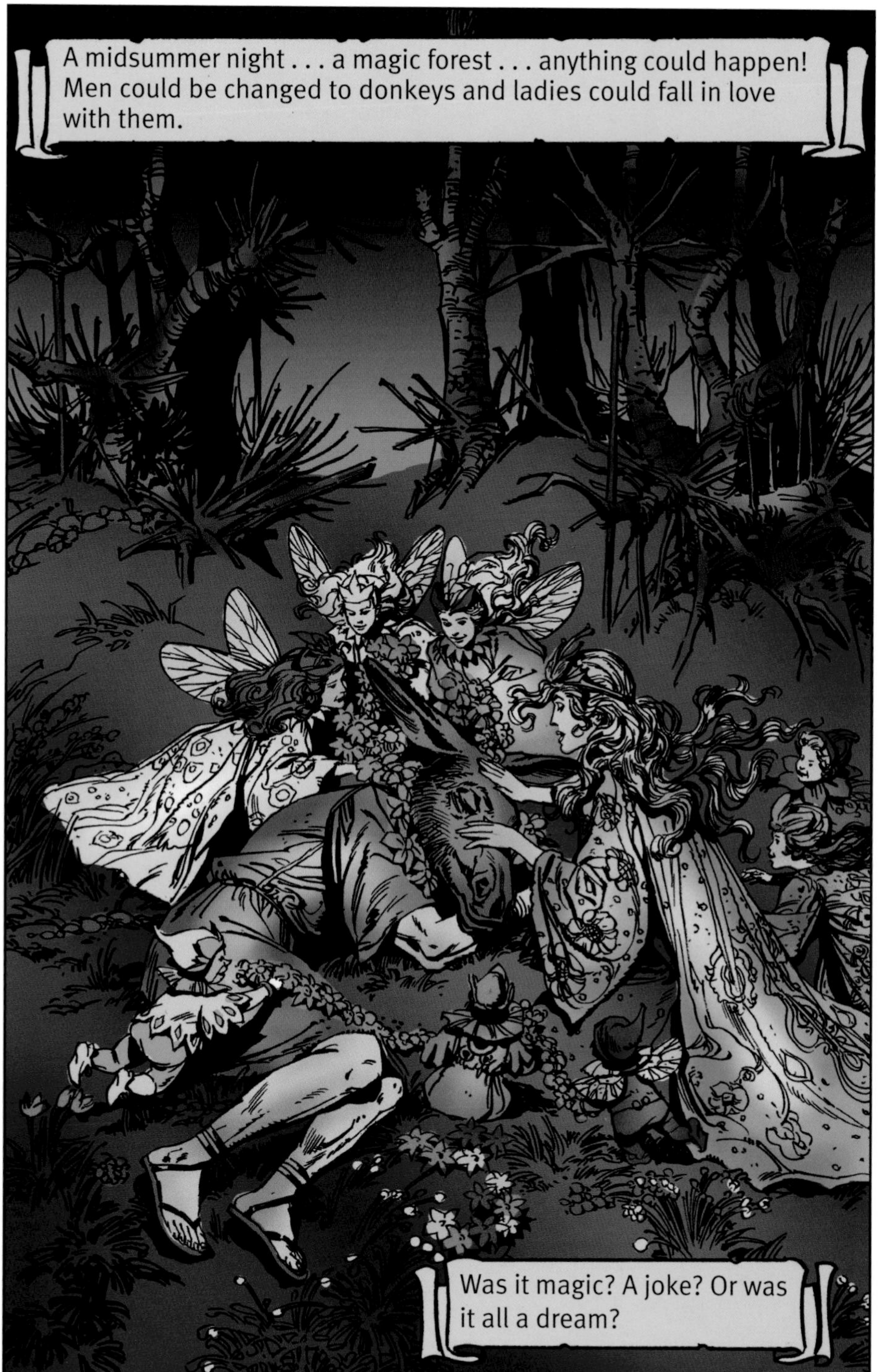
A midsummer night . . . a magic forest . . . anything could happen! Men could be changed to donkeys and ladies could fall in love with them.
Was it magic? A joke? Or was it all a dream?

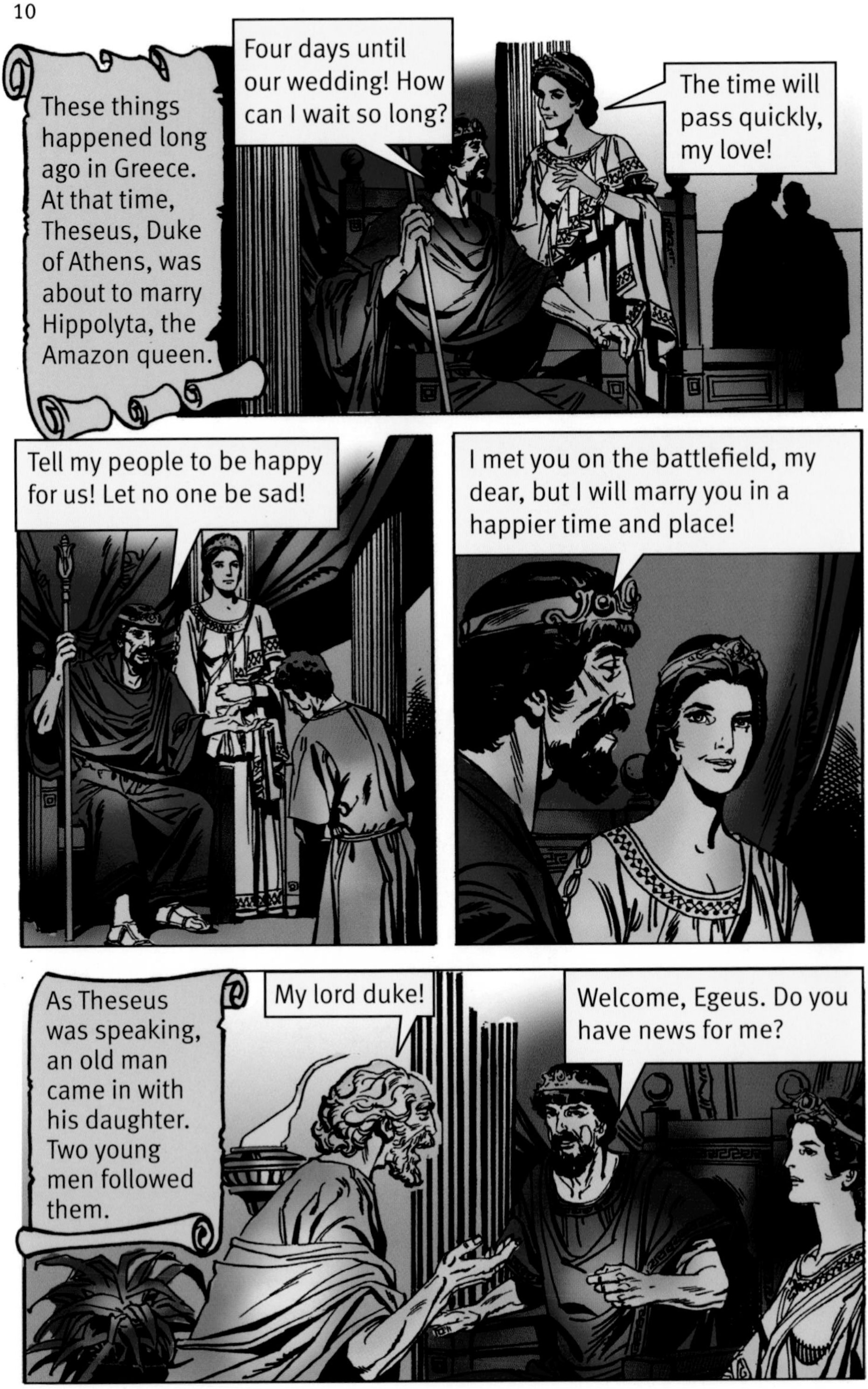
These things happened long ago in Greece. At that time, Theseus, Duke of Athens, was about to marry Hippolyta, the Amazon queen.
Four days until our wedding! How can I wait so long?
The time will pass quickly, my love!
Tell my people to be happy for us! Let no one be sad!
I met you on the battlefield, my dear, but I will marry you in a happier time and place!
As Theseus was speaking, an old man came in with his daughter. Two young men followed them.
My lord duke!
Welcome, Egeus. Do you have news for me?

Yes, sir. It is my daughter Hermia.

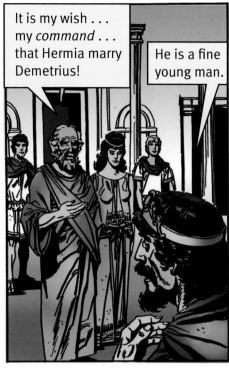

It is my wish . . . my *command* . . . that Hermia marry Demetrius!

He is a fine young man.

Besides, you must obey your father.

But I love Lysander, who is also a fine young man!

At first Demetrius loved my best friend, Helena. He won her heart, but now he wishes to break it—and mine—by marrying *me*!

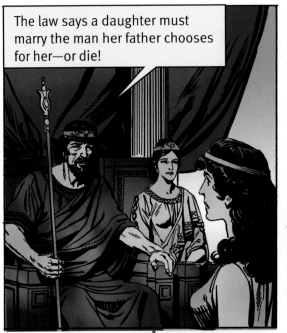

The law says a daughter must marry the man her father chooses for her—or die!

You have four days to think it over.

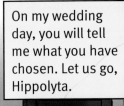

On my wedding day, you will tell me what you have chosen. Let us go, Hippolyta.

Soon the unhappy couple were left alone.

Don't look so sad, my love. I have a plan!

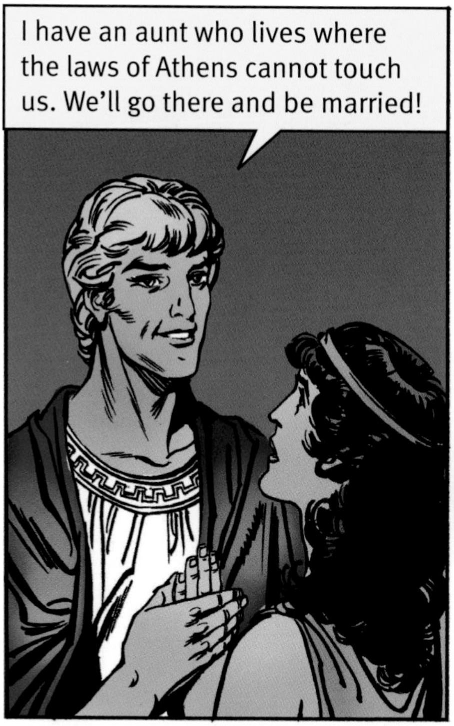
I have an aunt who lives where the laws of Athens cannot touch us. We'll go there and be married!

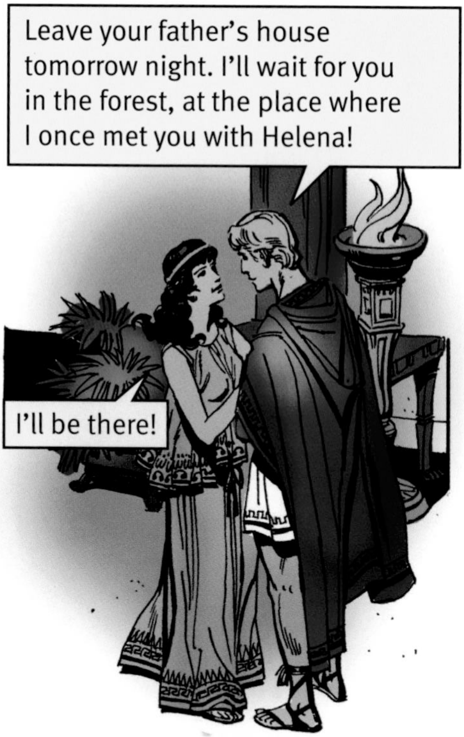
Leave your father's house tomorrow night. I'll wait for you in the forest, at the place where I once met you with Helena!
I'll be there!

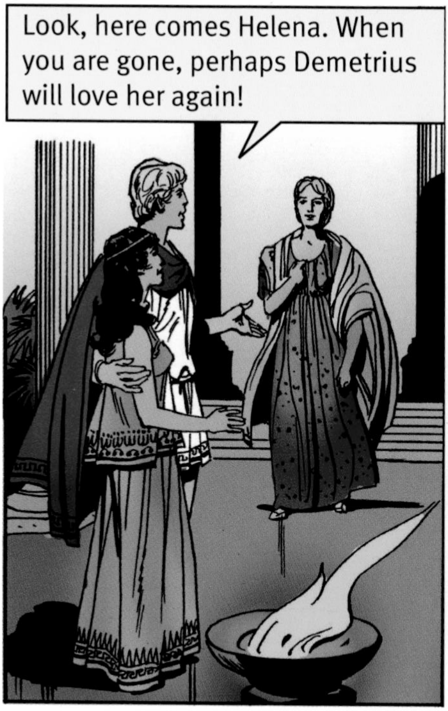
Look, here comes Helena. When you are gone, perhaps Demetrius will love her again!

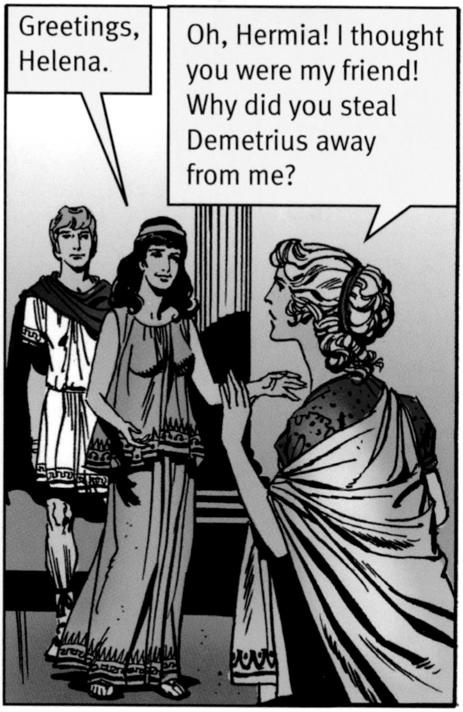
Greetings, Helena.
Oh, Hermia! I thought you were my friend! Why did you steal Demetrius away from me?

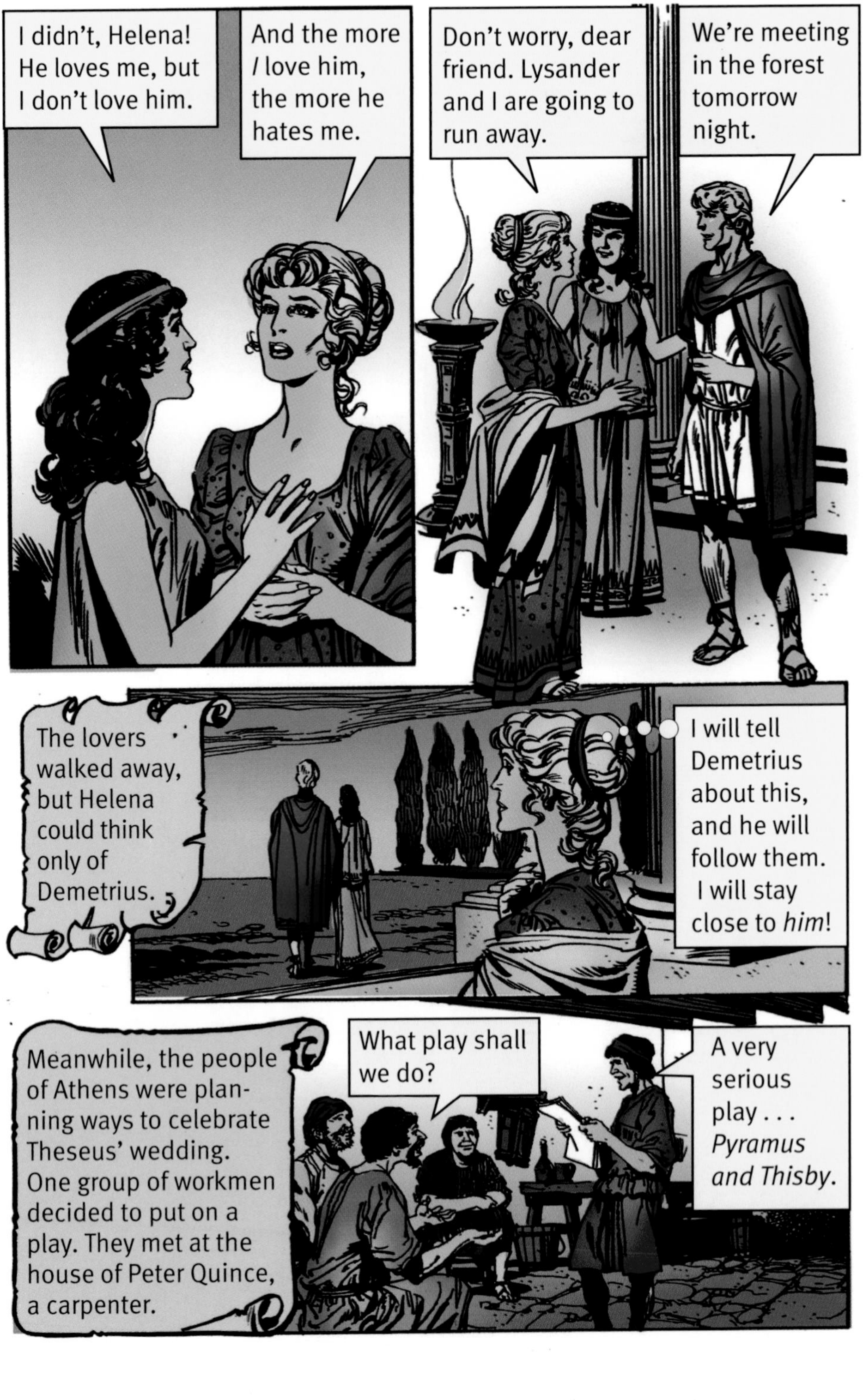
I didn't, Helena! He loves me, but I don't love him.
And the more *I* love him, the more he hates me.
Don't worry, dear friend. Lysander and I are going to run away.
We're meeting in the forest tomorrow night.
The lovers walked away, but Helena could think only of Demetrius.
I will tell Demetrius about this, and he will follow them. I will stay close to *him*!
Meanwhile, the people of Athens were planning ways to celebrate Theseus' wedding. One group of workmen decided to put on a play. They met at the house of Peter Quince, a carpenter.
What play shall we do?
A very serious play . . . *Pyramus and Thisby*.

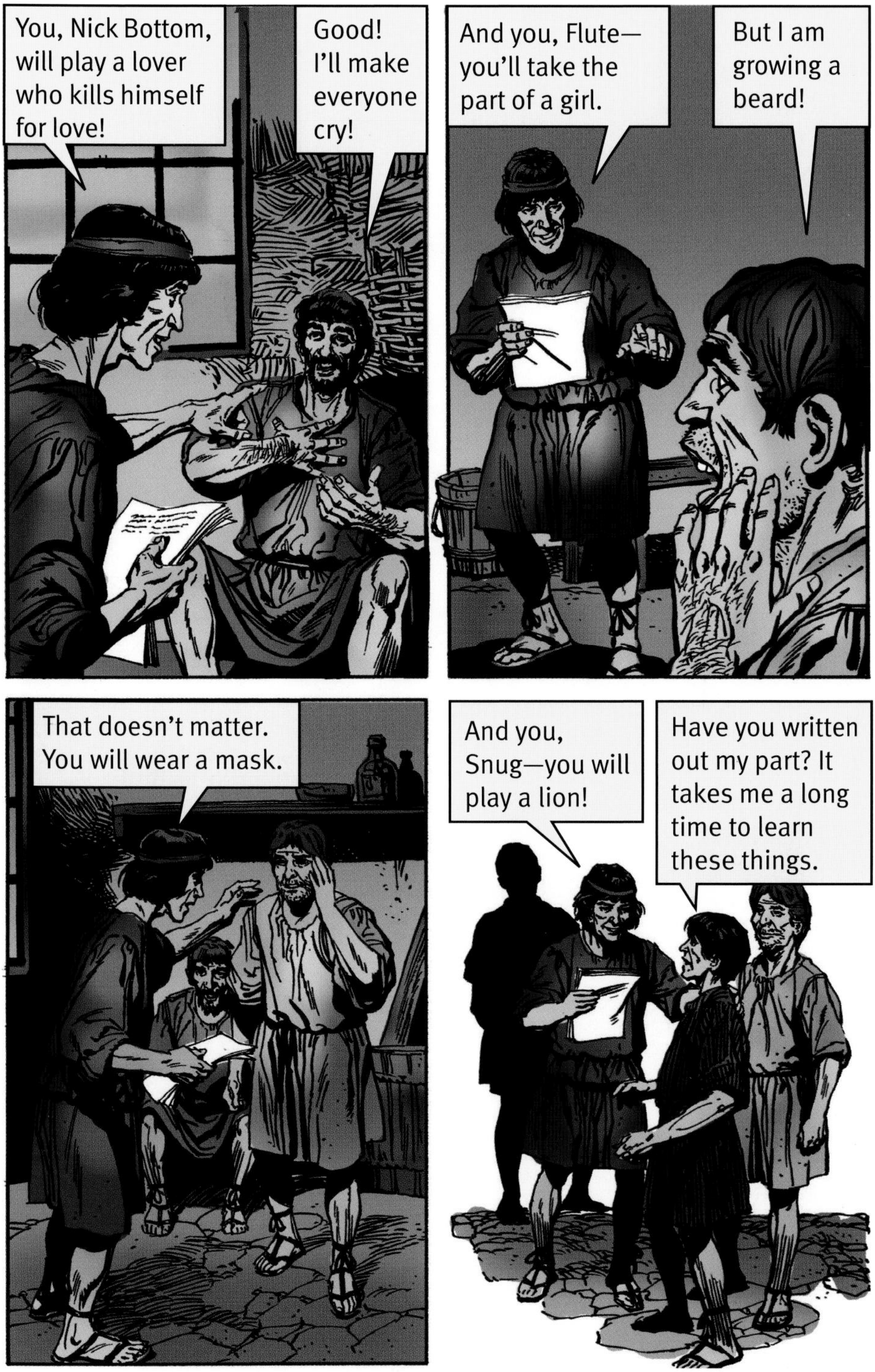
You, Nick Bottom, will play a lover who kills himself for love!
Good! I'll make everyone cry!
And you, Flute—you'll take the part of a girl.
But I am growing a beard!
That doesn't matter. You will wear a mask.
And you, Snug—you will play a lion!
Have you written out my part? It takes me a long time to learn these things.

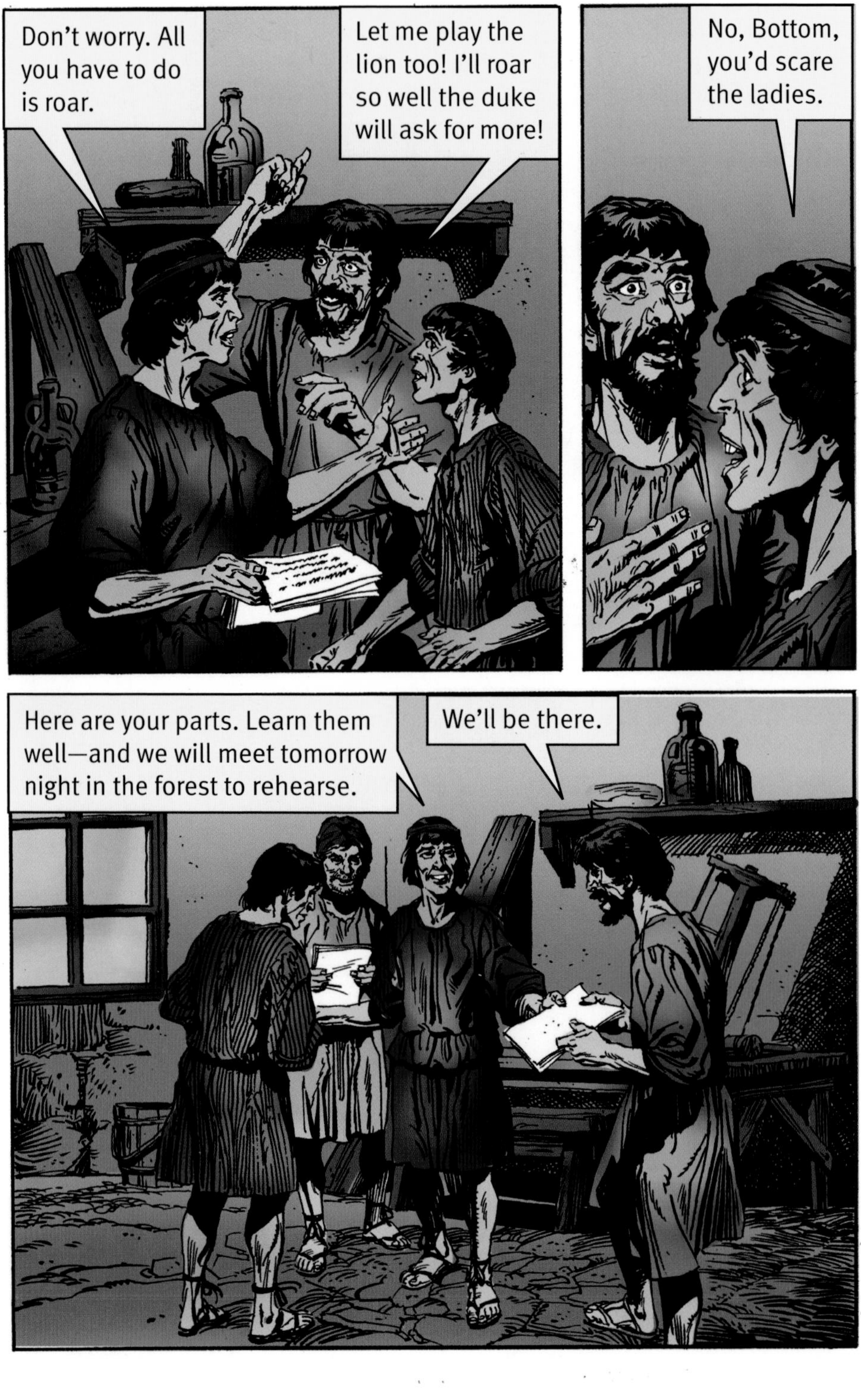
Don't worry. All you have to do is roar.
Let me play the lion too! I'll roar so well the duke will ask for more!
No, Bottom, you'd scare the ladies.
Here are your parts. Learn them well—and we will meet tomorrow night in the forest to rehearse.
We'll be there.

The next night, the young lovers went to the forest. So did the actors. But the elves and fairies were there ahead of them.

Where are you going, Spirit?

Wherever my fairy queen Titania tells me to go!

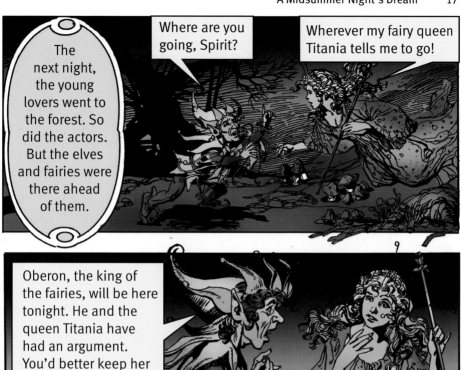

Oberon, the king of the fairies, will be here tonight. He and the queen Titania have had an argument. You'd better keep her away from here!

Titania has a lovely servant boy whom she stole from an Indian king. Oberon wants the boy as his *own* servant.

But the queen will not give him up. Oberon is very angry!

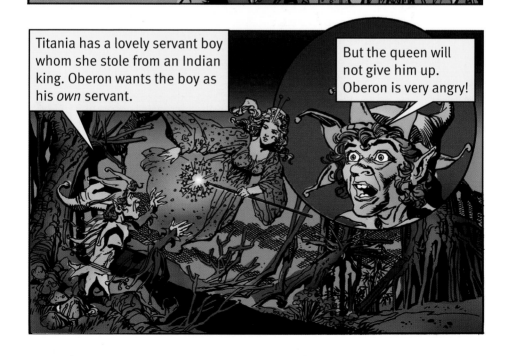

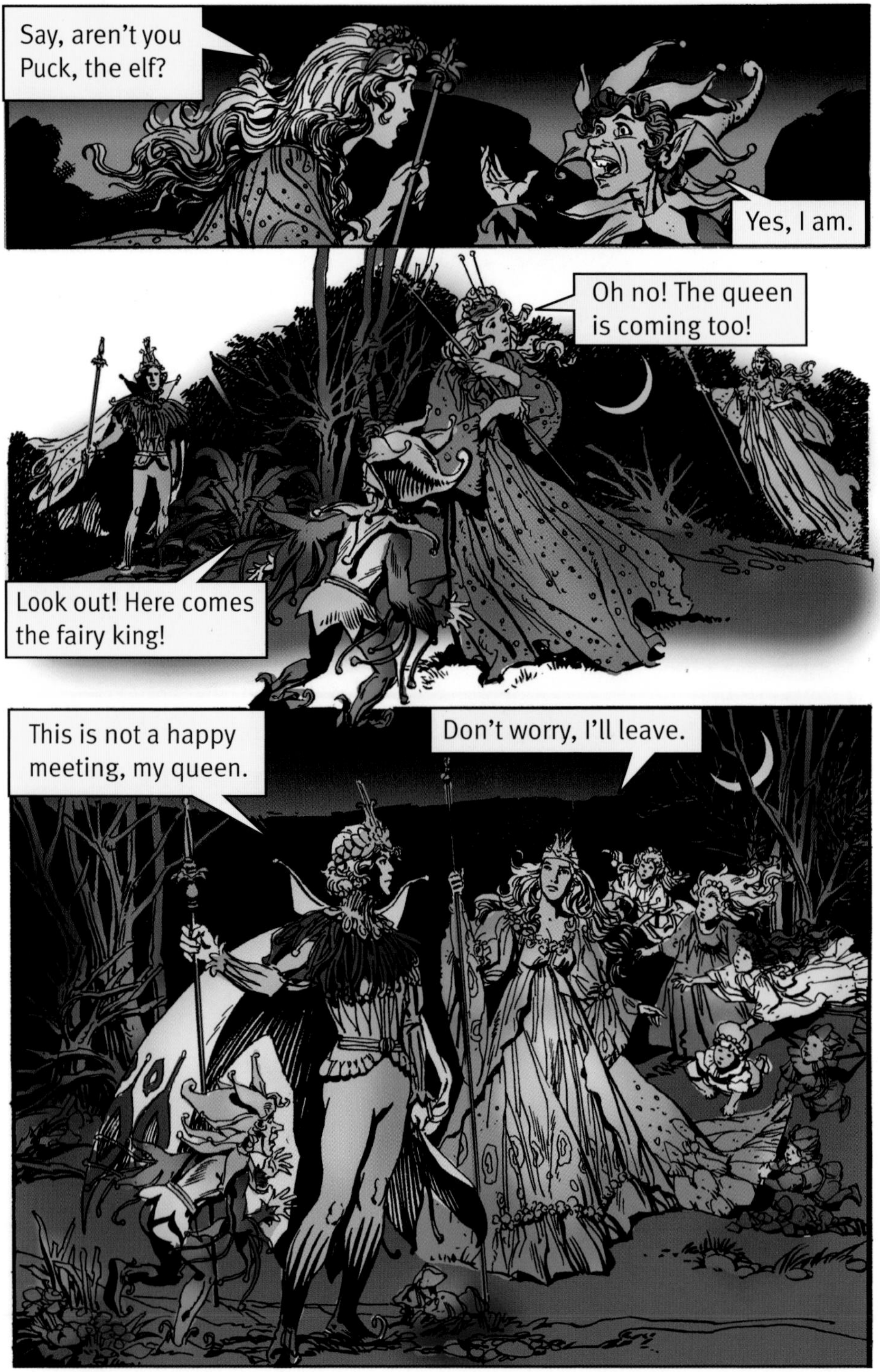
Say, aren't you Puck, the elf?
Yes, I am.
Oh no! The queen is coming too!
Look out! Here comes the fairy king!
This is not a happy meeting, my queen.
Don't worry, I'll leave.

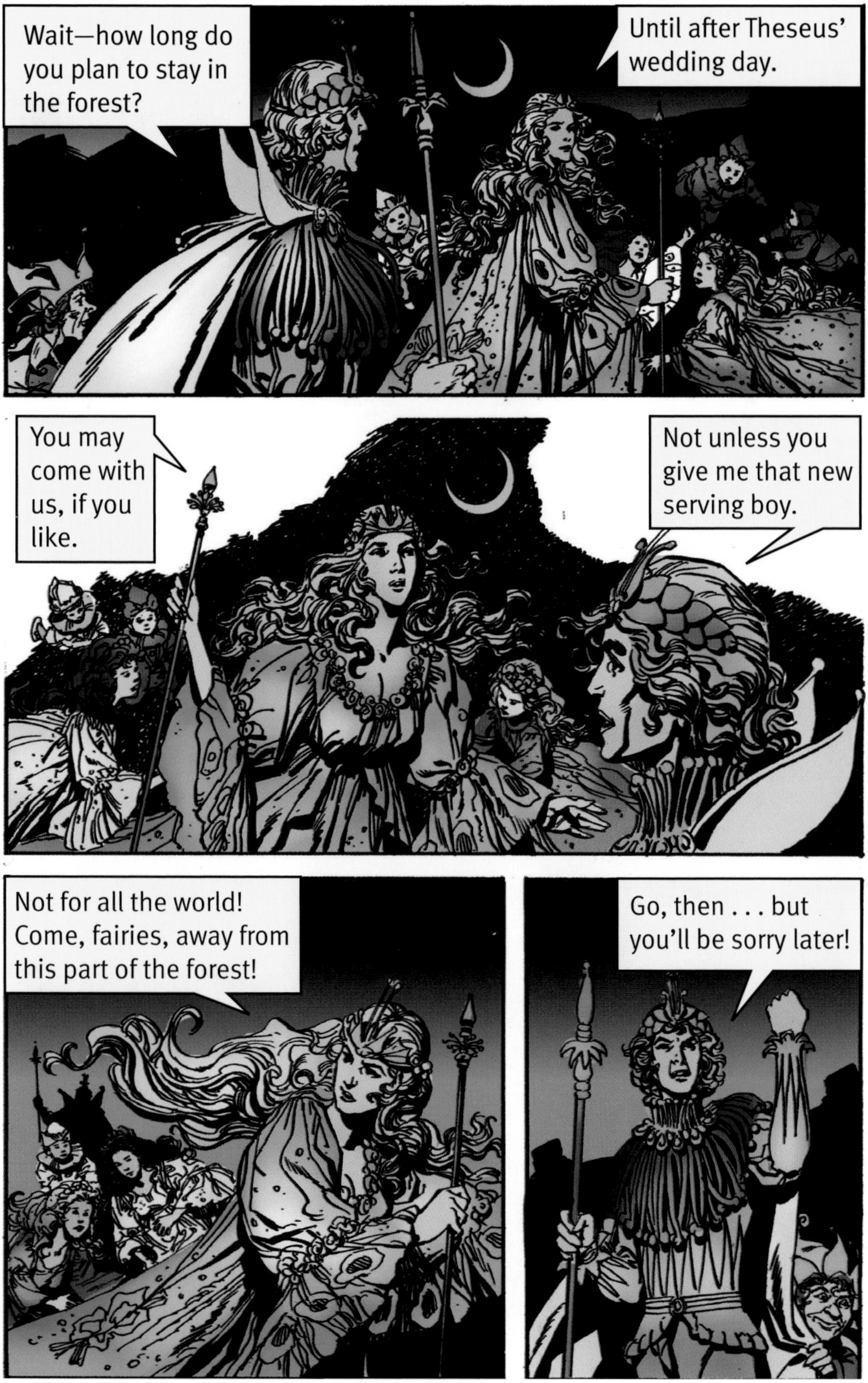
Wait—how long do you plan to stay in the forest?
Until after Theseus' wedding day.
You may come with us, if you like.
Not unless you give me that new serving boy.
Not for all the world! Come, fairies, away from this part of the forest!
Go, then . . . but you'll be sorry later!

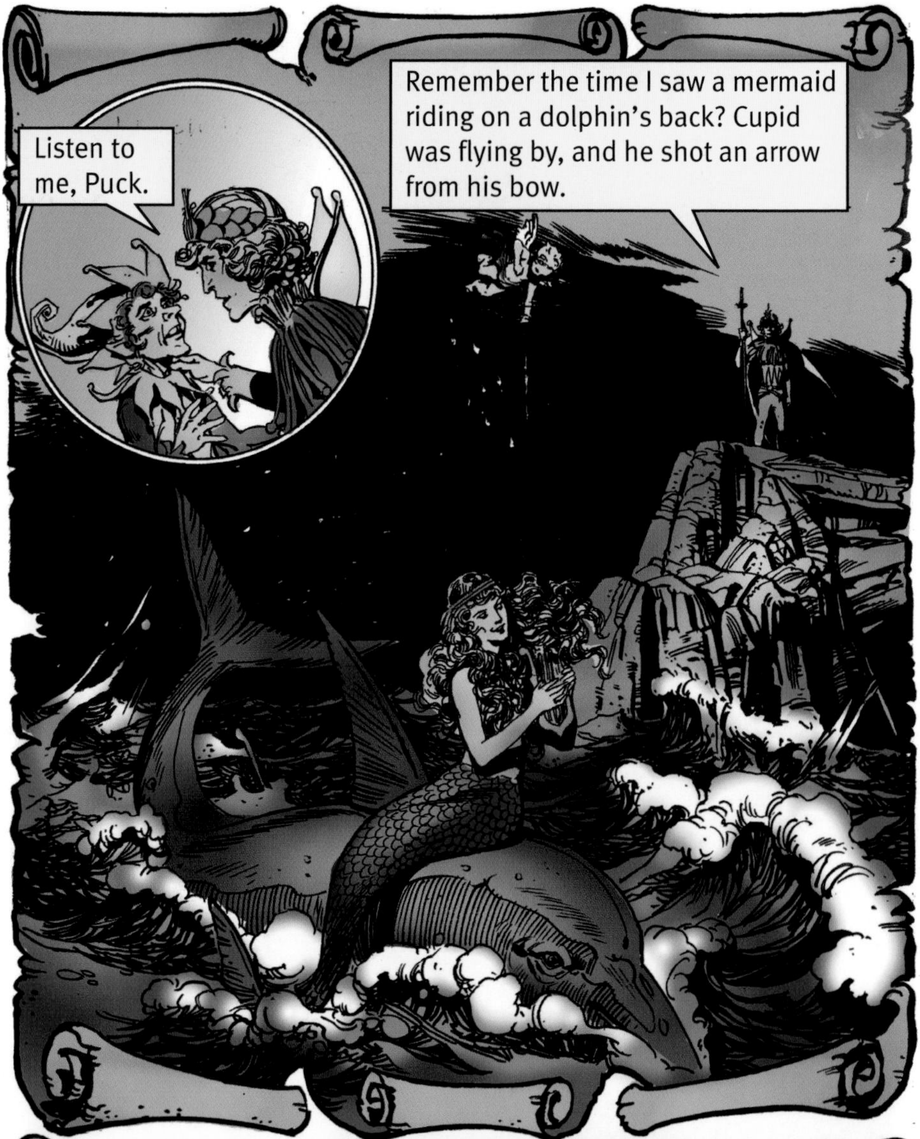
Listen to me, Puck.
Remember the time I saw a mermaid riding on a dolphin's back? Cupid was flying by, and he shot an arrow from his bow.

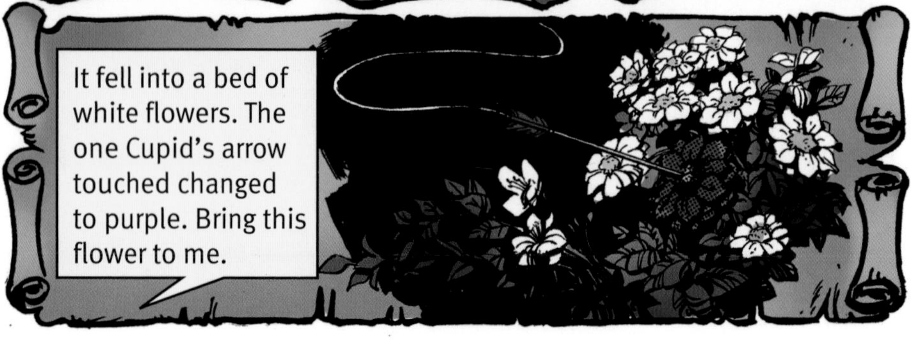
It fell into a bed of white flowers. The one Cupid's arrow touched changed to purple. Bring this flower to me.

Its magic juice will make a sleeping person fall in love with the first creature he sees when he awakes.

I'll be back in a flash!

I'll put some on Titania's eyes tonight. And I won't remove the spell until she gives me the boy!

I hear human voices! Since I am invisible to them, I'll stay and listen!

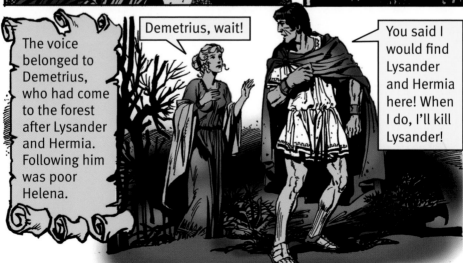

The voice belonged to Demetrius, who had come to the forest after Lysander and Hermia. Following him was poor Helena.

Demetrius, wait!

You said I would find Lysander and Hermia here! When I do, I'll kill Lysander!

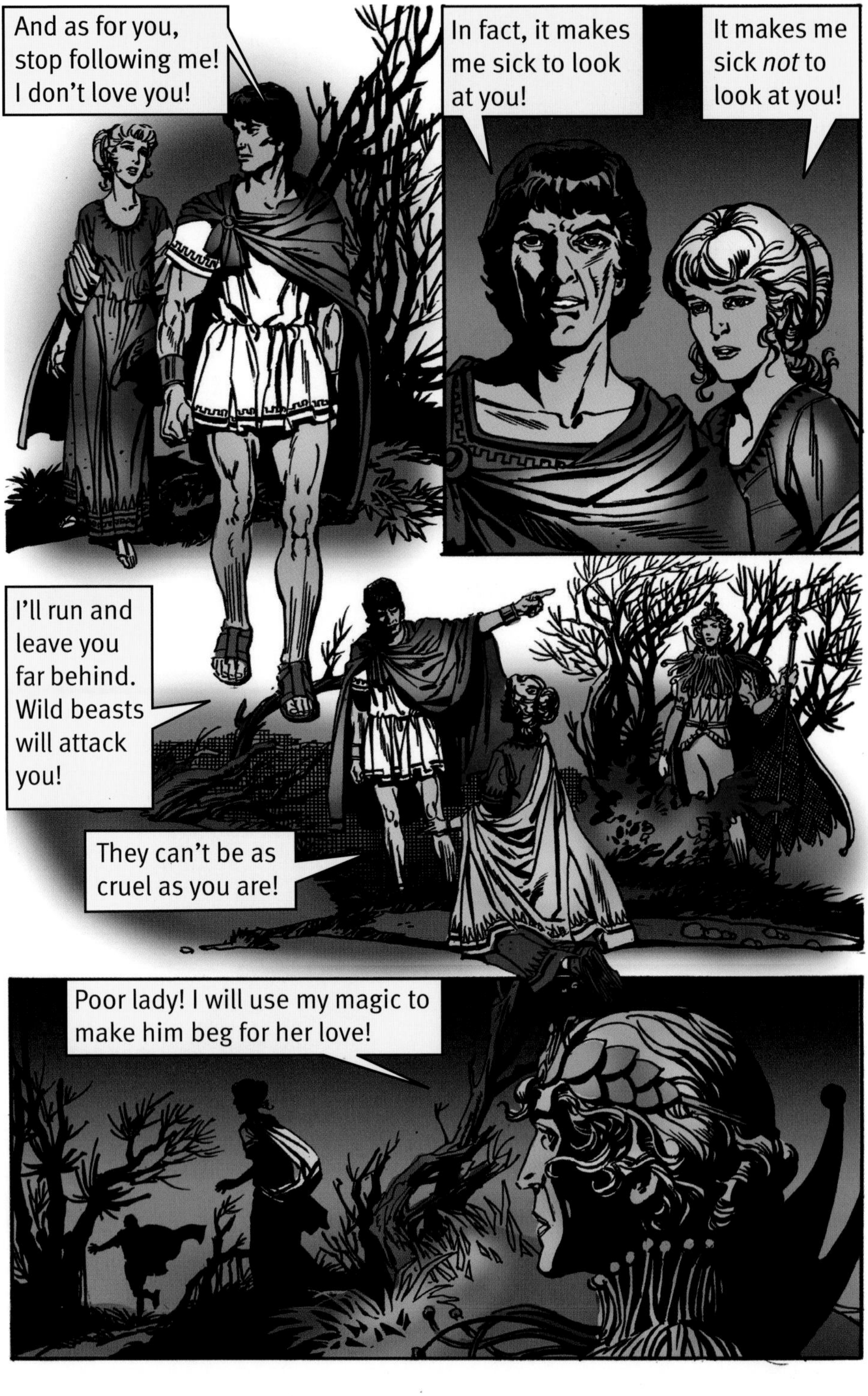
And as for you, stop following me! I don't love you!
In fact, it makes me sick to look at you!
It makes me sick *not* to look at you!
I'll run and leave you far behind. Wild beasts will attack you!
They can't be as cruel as you are!
Poor lady! I will use my magic to make him beg for her love!

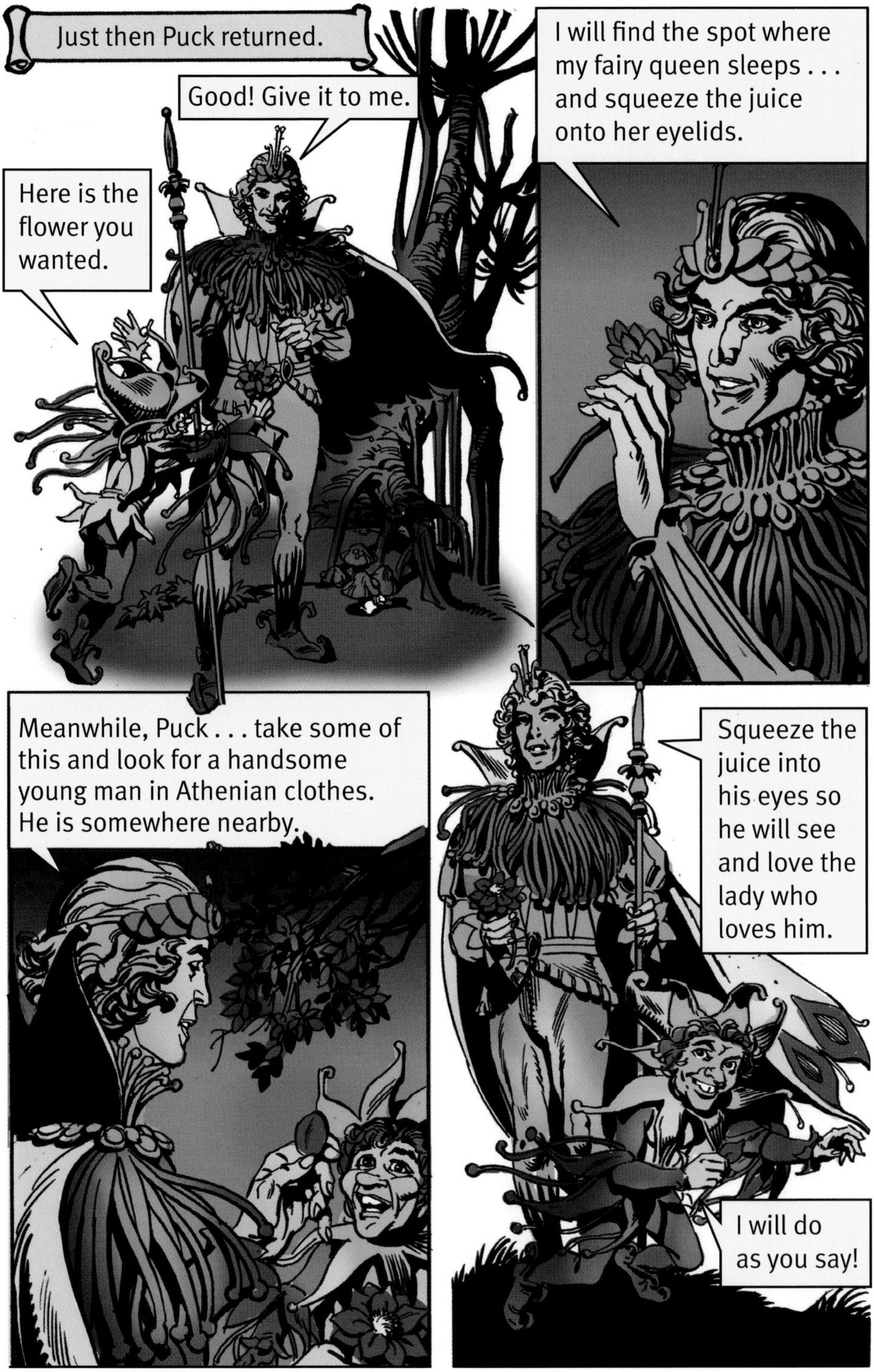
Just then Puck returned.
Here is the flower you wanted.
Good! Give it to me.
I will find the spot where my fairy queen sleeps . . . and squeeze the juice onto her eyelids.
Meanwhile, Puck . . . take some of this and look for a handsome young man in Athenian clothes. He is somewhere nearby.
Squeeze the juice into his eyes so he will see and love the lady who loves him.
I will do as you say!

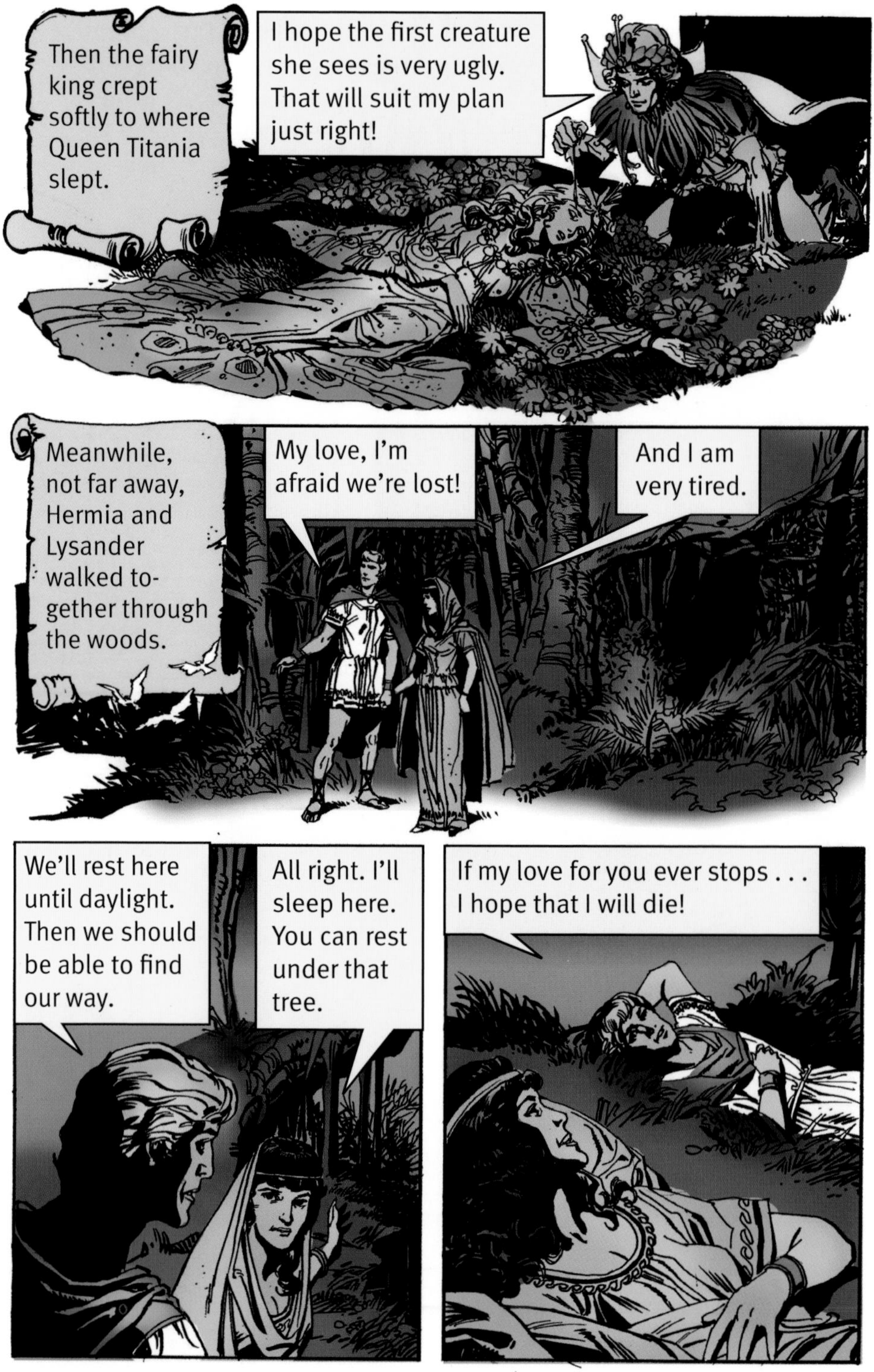
Then the fairy king crept softly to where Queen Titania slept.
I hope the first creature she sees is very ugly. That will suit my plan just right!
Meanwhile, not far away, Hermia and Lysander walked to-gether through the woods.
My love, I'm afraid we're lost!
And I am very tired.
We'll rest here until daylight. Then we should be able to find our way.
All right. I'll sleep here. You can rest under that tree.
If my love for you ever stops . . . I hope that I will die!

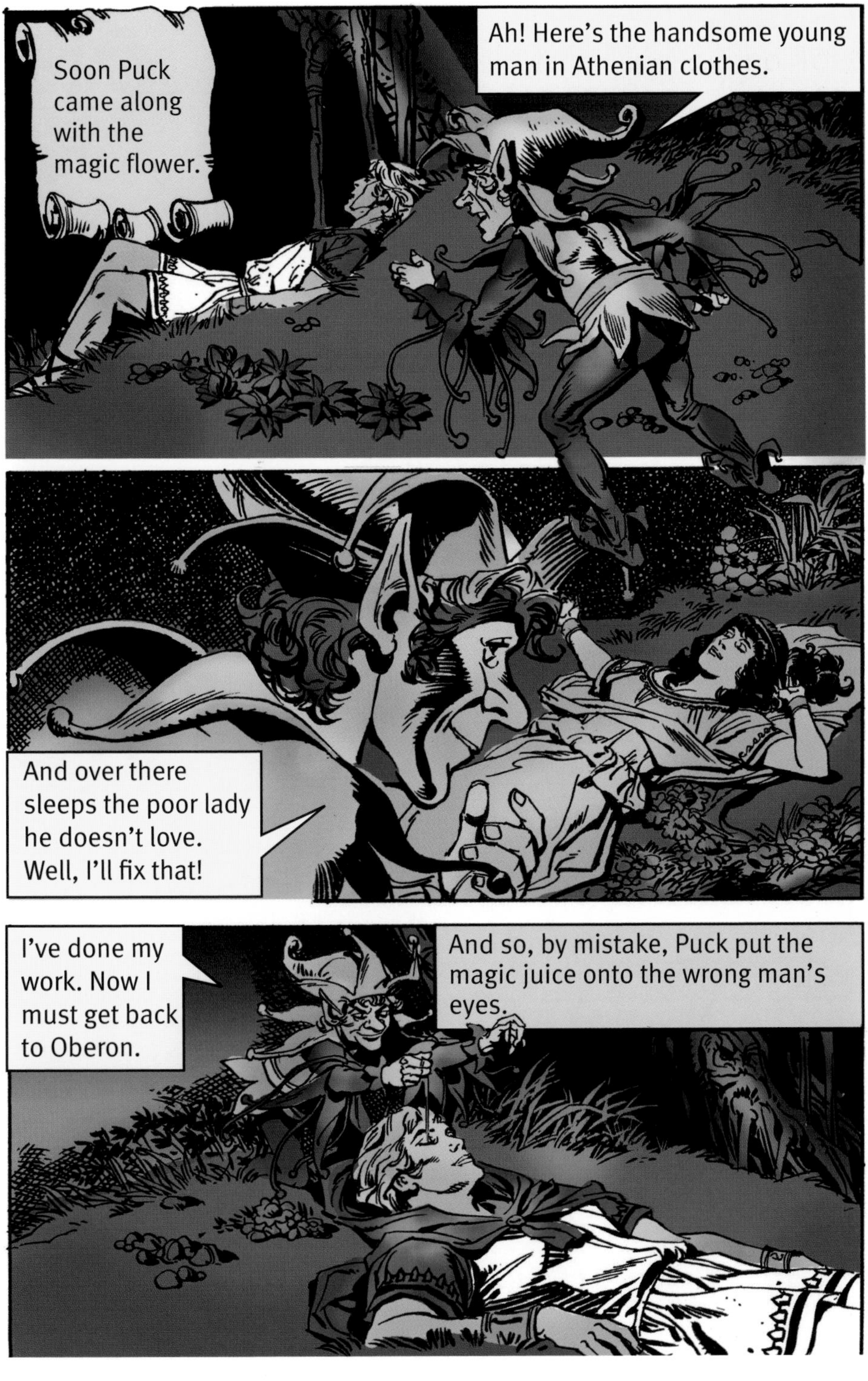
Soon Puck came along with the magic flower.
Ah! Here's the handsome young man in Athenian clothes.
And over there sleeps the poor lady he doesn't love. Well, I'll fix that!
I've done my work. Now I must get back to Oberon.
And so, by mistake, Puck put the magic juice onto the wrong man's eyes.

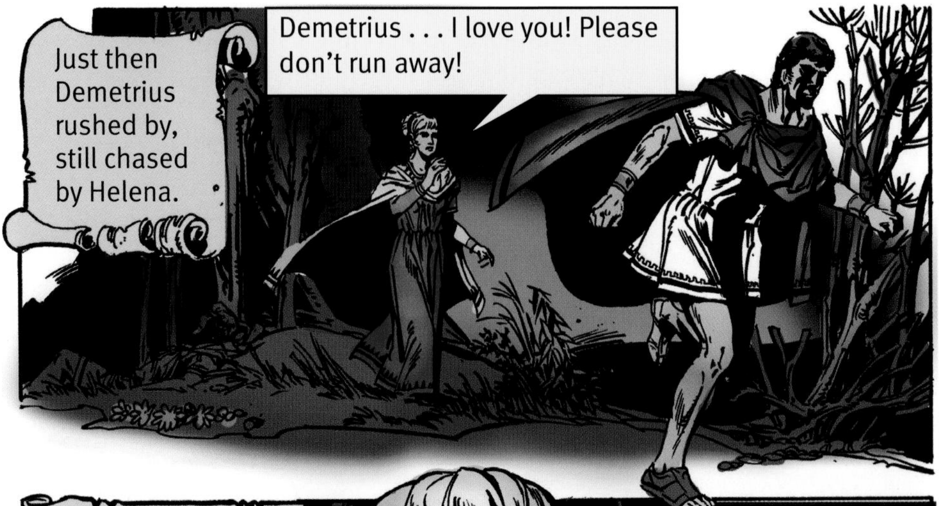
Just then Demetrius rushed by, still chased by Helena.
Demetrius . . . I love you! Please don't run away!

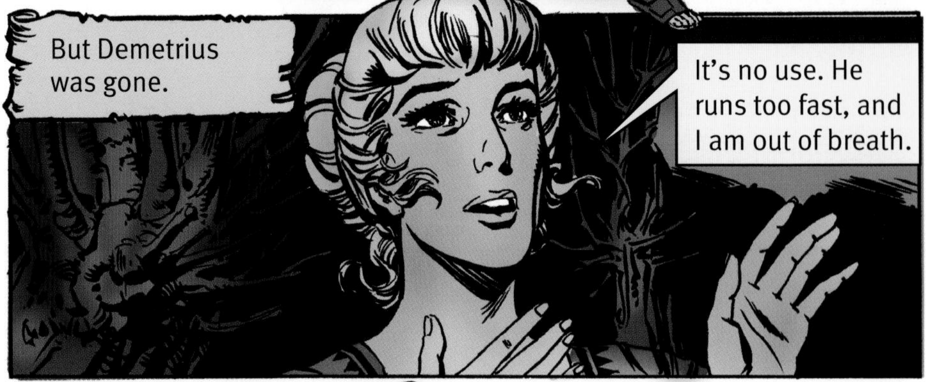
But Demetrius was gone.
It's no use. He runs too fast, and I am out of breath.

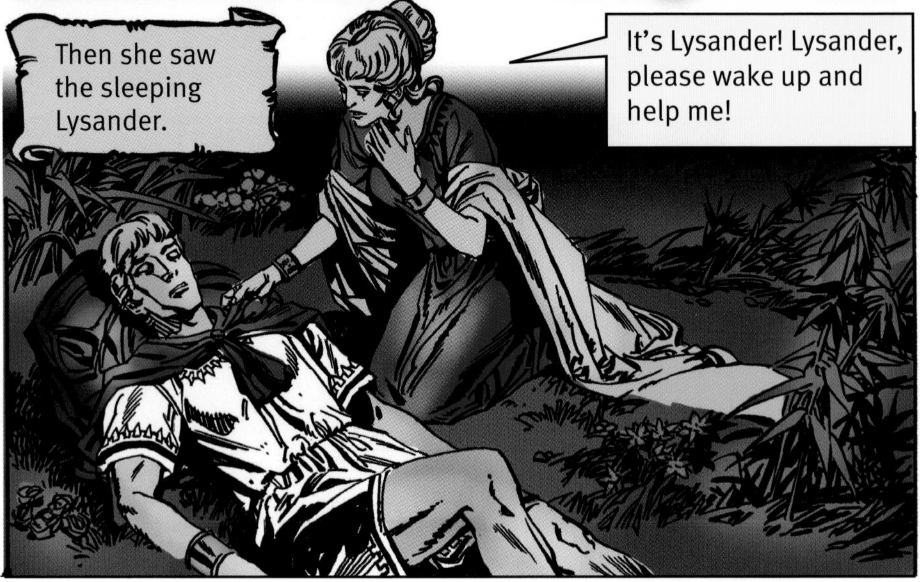
Then she saw the sleeping Lysander.
It's Lysander! Lysander, please wake up and help me!

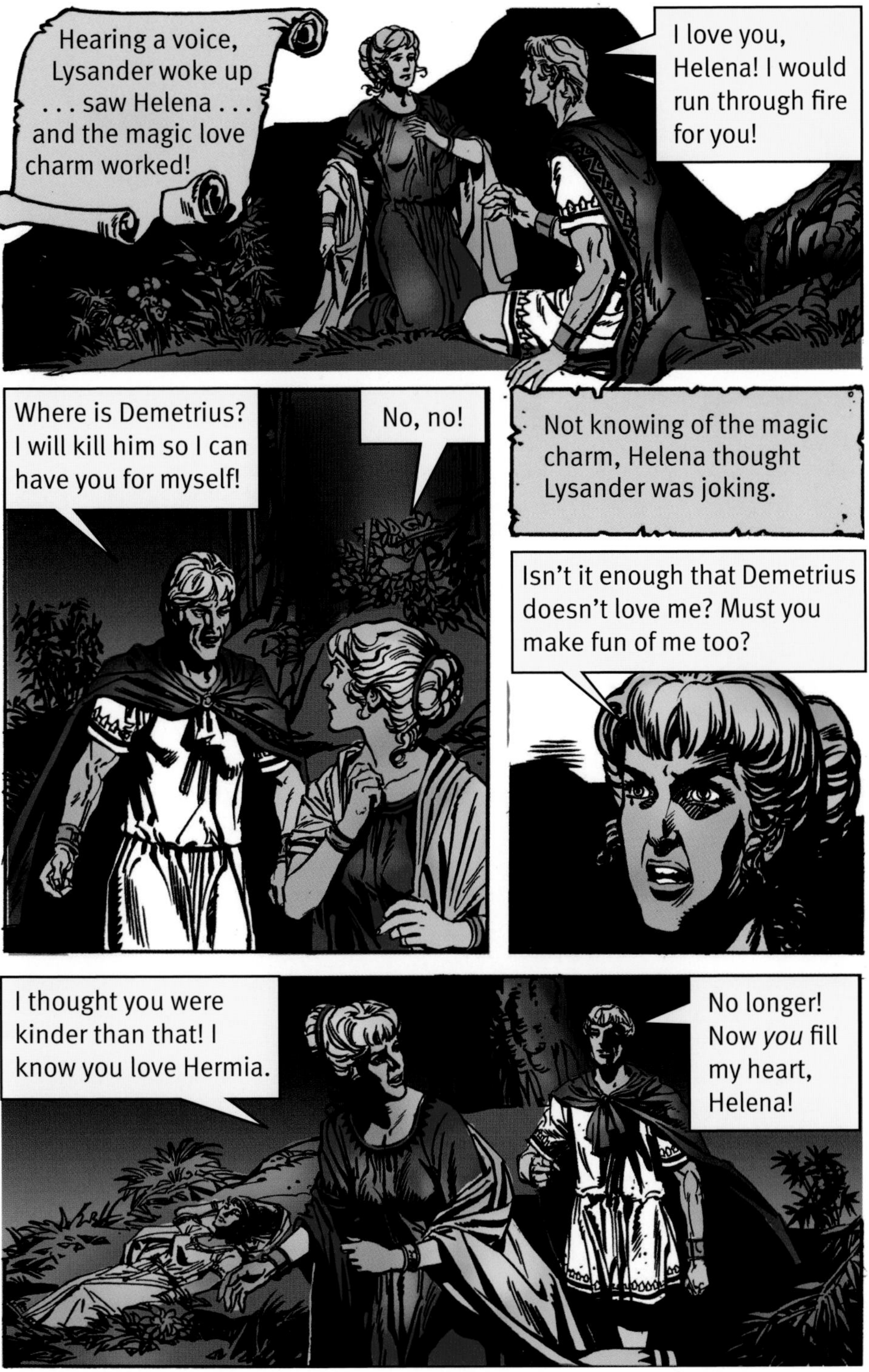
Hearing a voice, Lysander woke up . . . saw Helena . . . and the magic love charm worked!
I love you, Helena! I would run through fire for you!
Where is Demetrius? I will kill him so I can have you for myself!
No, no!
Not knowing of the magic charm, Helena thought Lysander was joking.
Isn't it enough that Demetrius doesn't love me? Must you make fun of me too?
I thought you were kinder than that! I know you love Hermia.
No longer! Now *you* fill my heart, Helena!

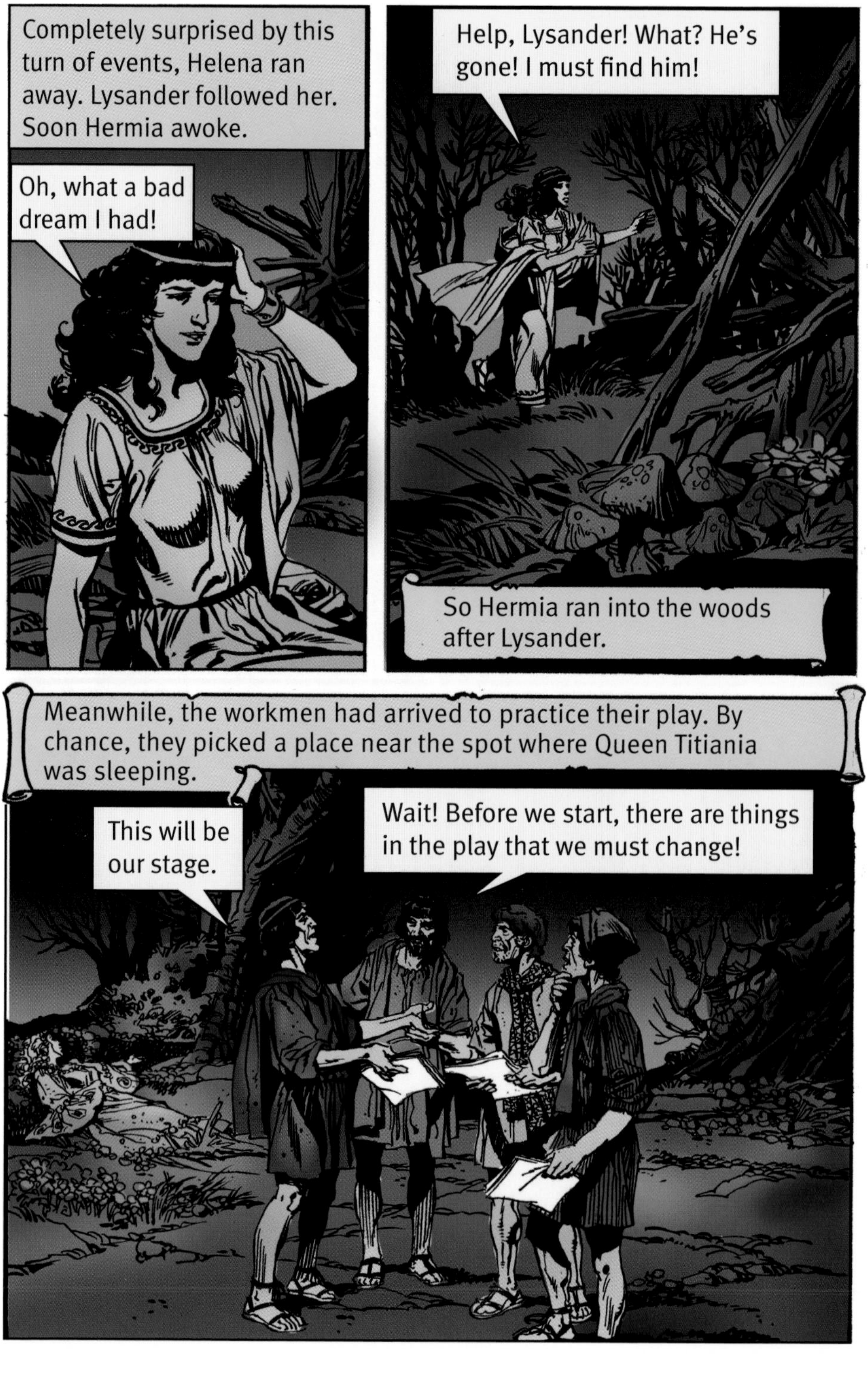
Completely surprised by this turn of events, Helena ran away. Lysander followed her. Soon Hermia awoke.
Oh, what a bad dream I had!
Help, Lysander! What? He's gone! I must find him!
So Hermia ran into the woods after Lysander.
Meanwhile, the workmen had arrived to practice their play. By chance, they picked a place near the spot where Queen Titiania was sleeping.
This will be our stage.
Wait! Before we start, there are things in the play that we must change!

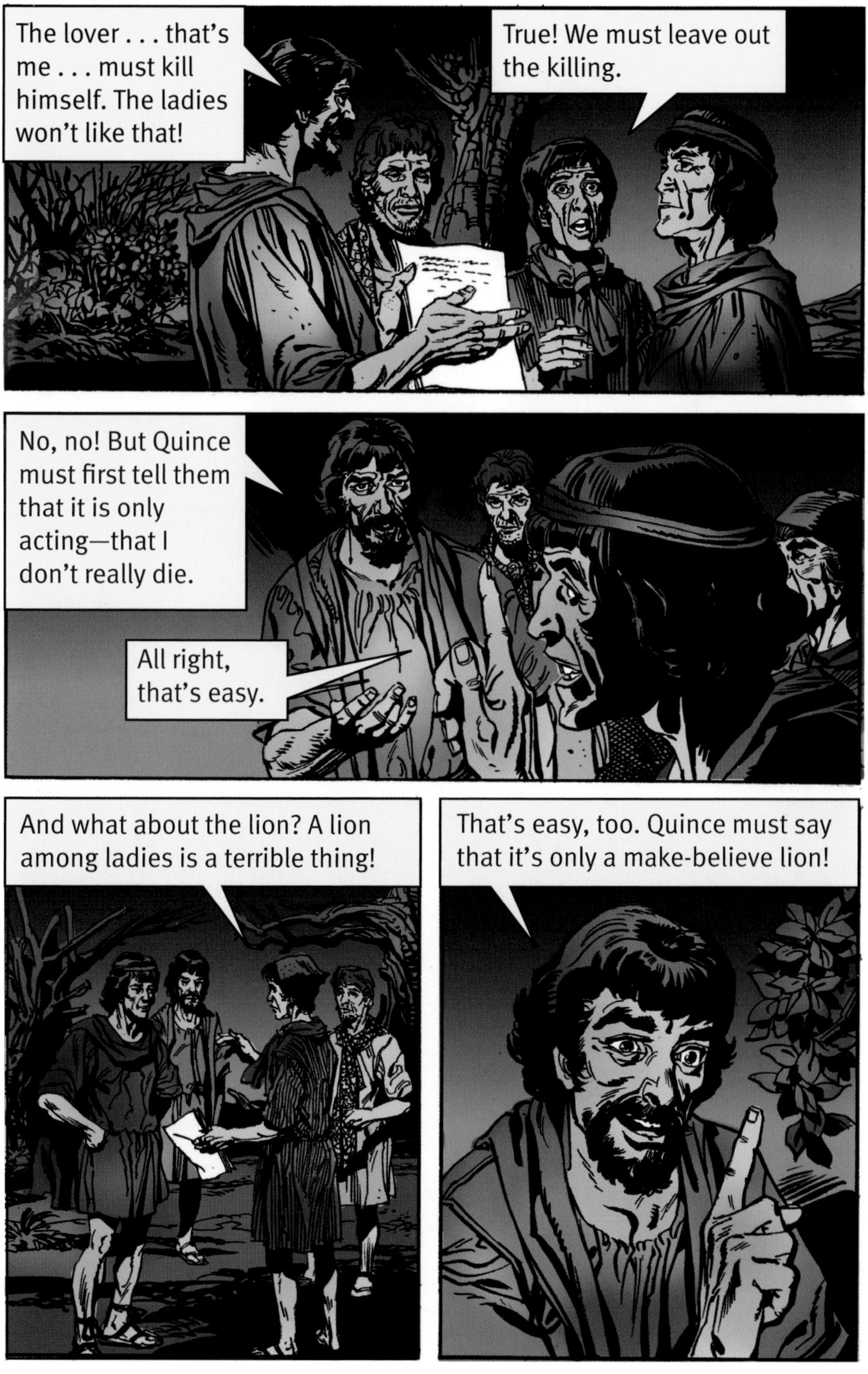
The lover . . . that's me . . . must kill himself. The ladies won't like that!
True! We must leave out the killing.
No, no! But Quince must first tell them that it is only acting—that I don't really die.
All right, that's easy.
And what about the lion? A lion among ladies is a terrible thing!
That's easy, too. Quince must say that it's only a make-believe lion!

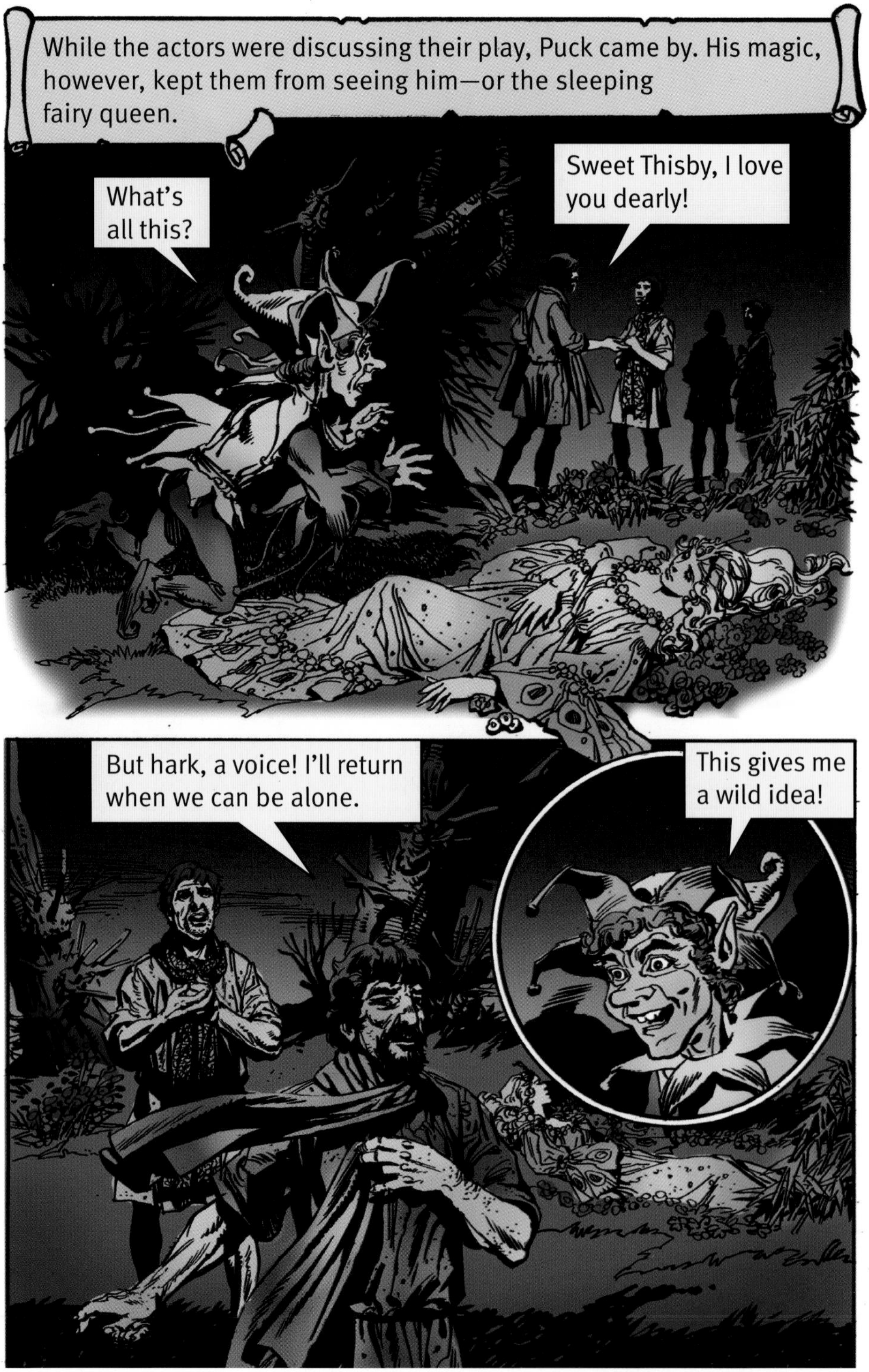
While the actors were discussing their play, Puck came by. His magic, however, kept them from seeing him—or the sleeping fairy queen.
What's all this?
Sweet Thisby, I love you dearly!
But hark, a voice! I'll return when we can be alone.
This gives me a wild idea!

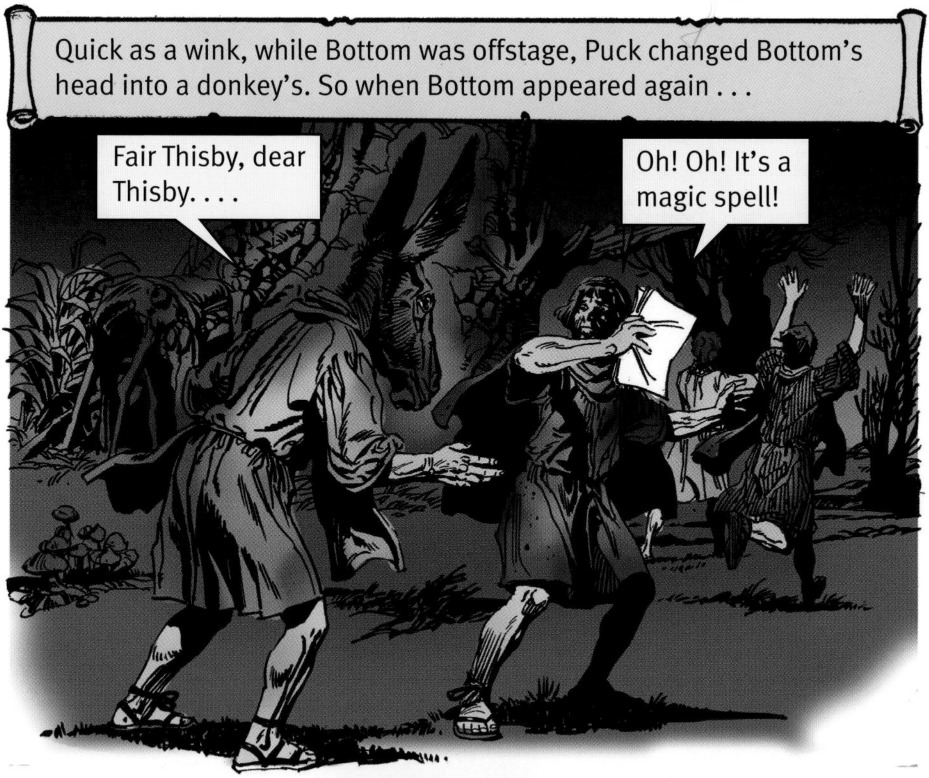
Quick as a wink, while Bottom was offstage, Puck changed Bottom's head into a donkey's. So when Bottom appeared again . . .
Fair Thisby, dear Thisby. . . .
Oh! Oh! It's a magic spell!

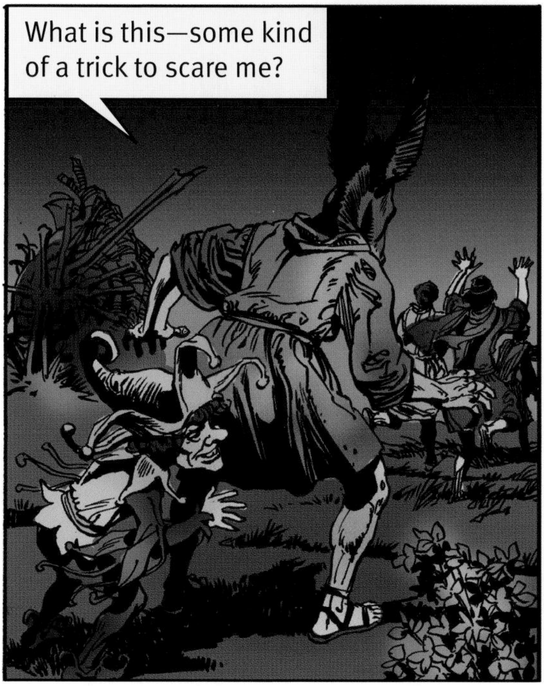
What is this—some kind of a trick to scare me?

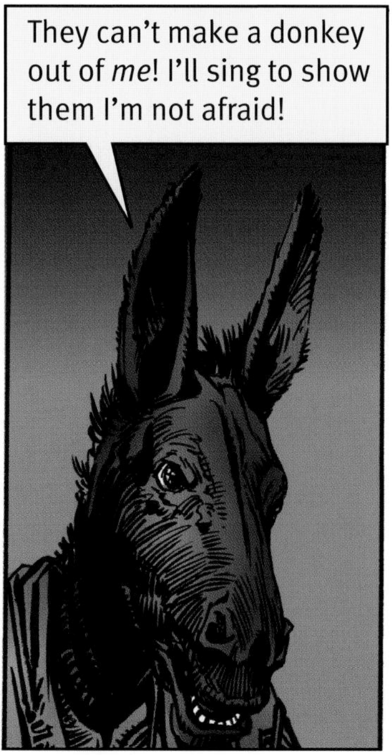
They can't make a donkey out of *me*! I'll sing to show them I'm not afraid!

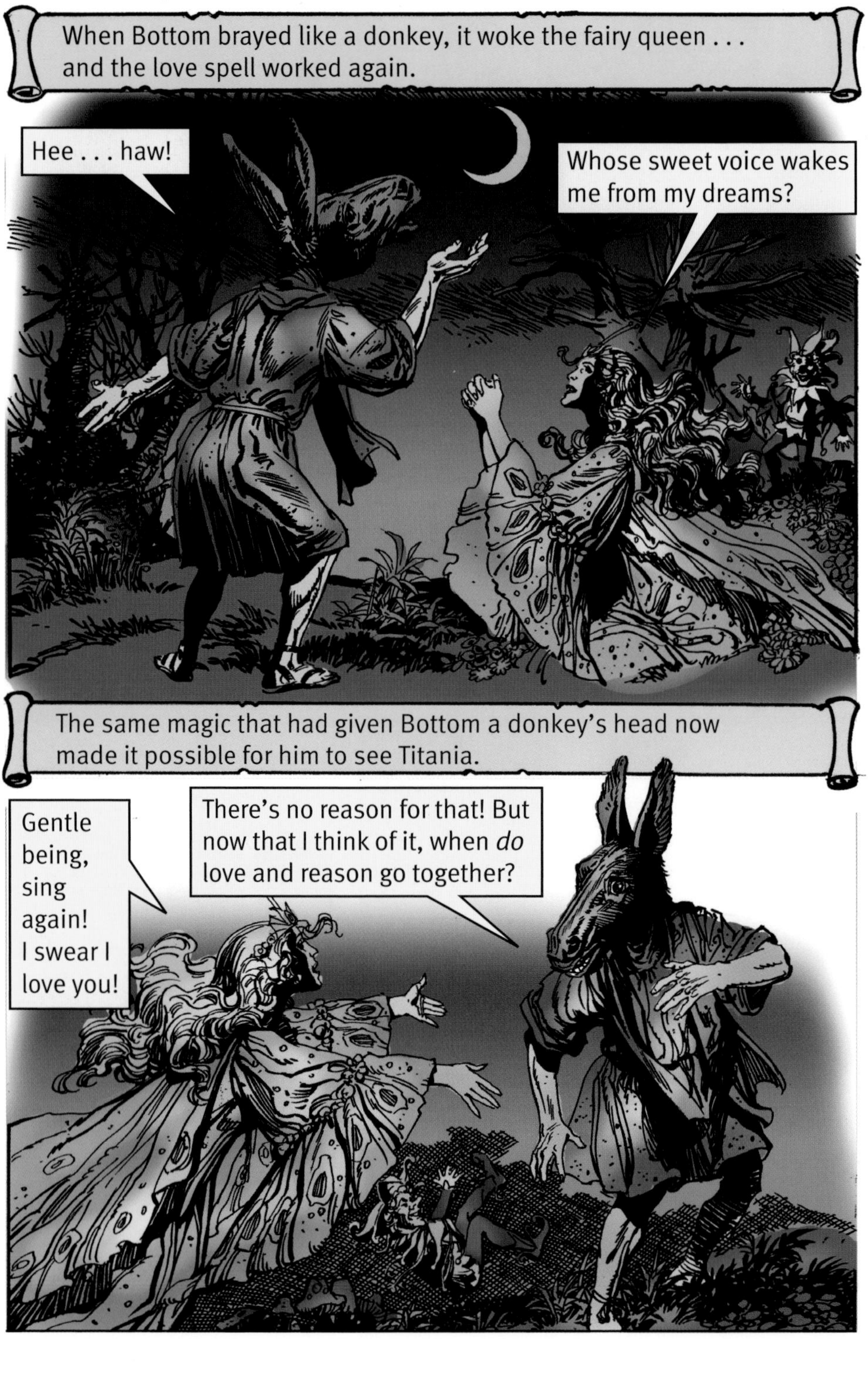
When Bottom brayed like a donkey, it woke the fairy queen . . . and the love spell worked again.
Hee . . . haw!
Whose sweet voice wakes me from my dreams?
The same magic that had given Bottom a donkey's head now made it possible for him to see Titania.
Gentle being, sing again! I swear I love you!
There's no reason for that! But now that I think of it, when *do* love and reason go together?

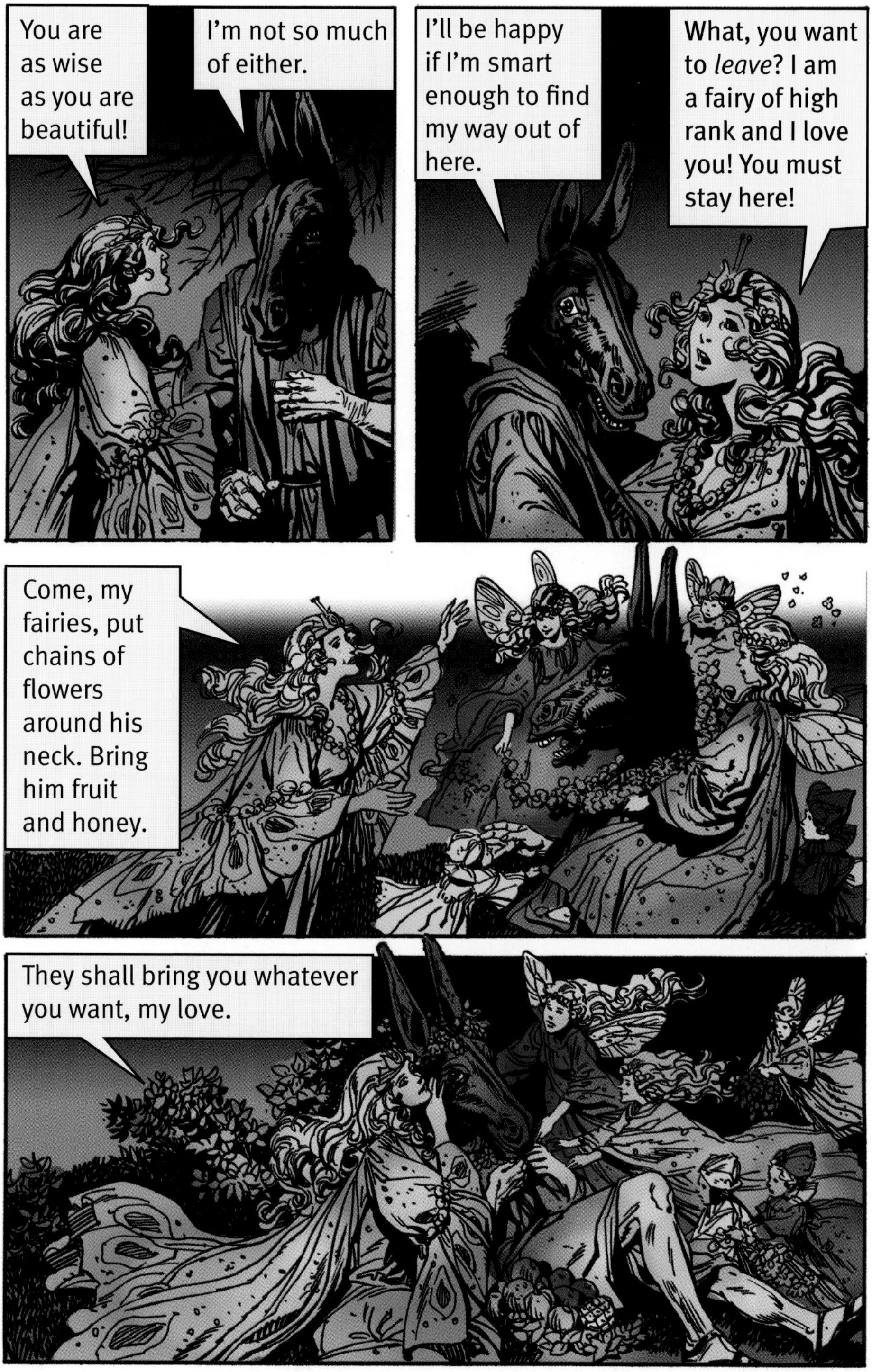
You are as wise as you are beautiful!
I'm not so much of either.
I'll be happy if I'm smart enough to find my way out of here.
What, you want to *leave*? I am a fairy of high rank and I love you! You must stay here!
Come, my fairies, put chains of flowers around his neck. Bring him fruit and honey.
They shall bring you whatever you want, my love.

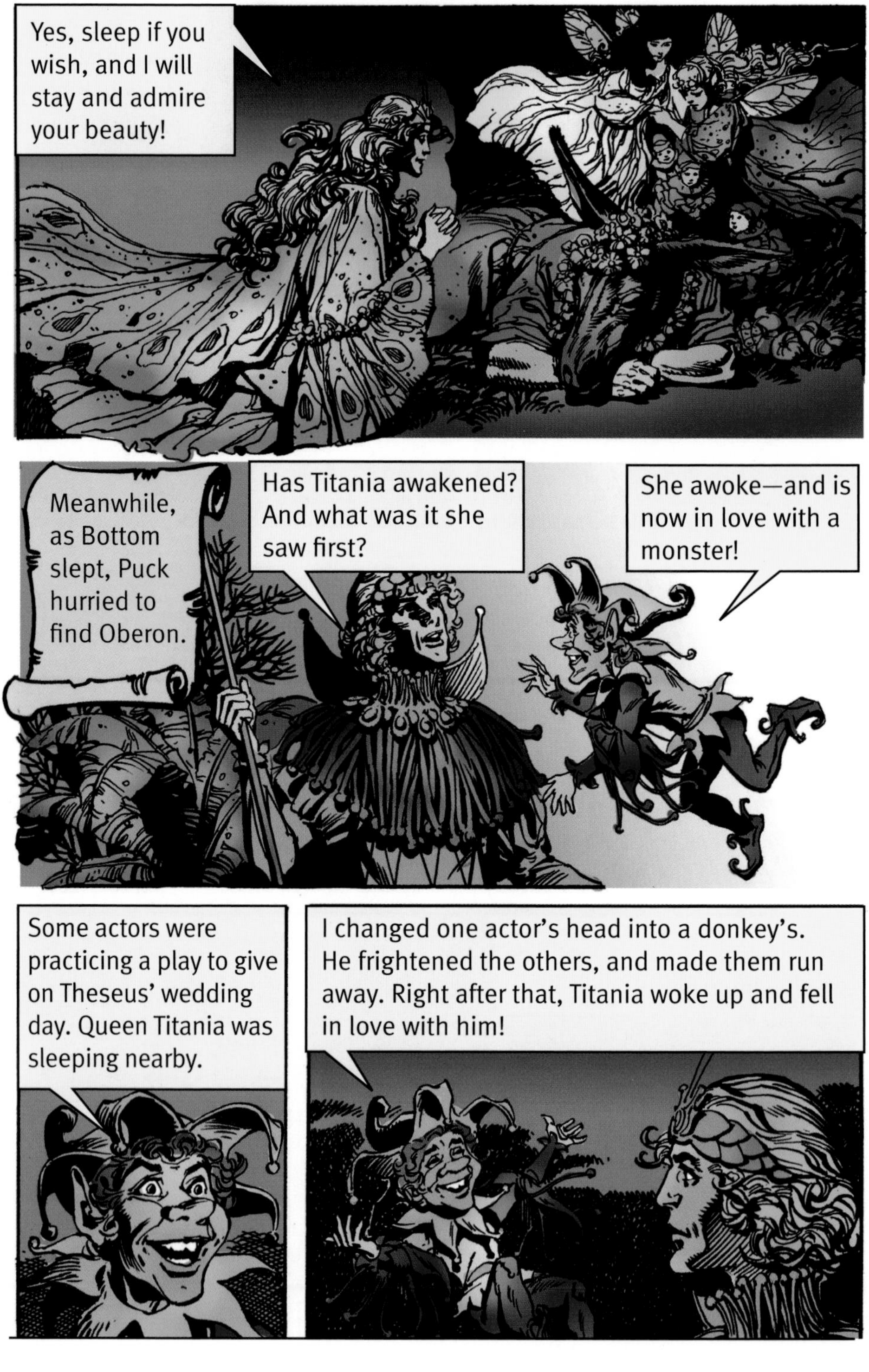
Yes, sleep if you wish, and I will stay and admire your beauty!
Meanwhile, as Bottom slept, Puck hurried to find Oberon.
Has Titania awakened? And what was it she saw first?
She awoke—and is now in love with a monster!
Some actors were practicing a play to give on Theseus' wedding day. Queen Titania was sleeping nearby.
I changed one actor's head into a donkey's. He frightened the others, and made them run away. Right after that, Titania woke up and fell in love with him!

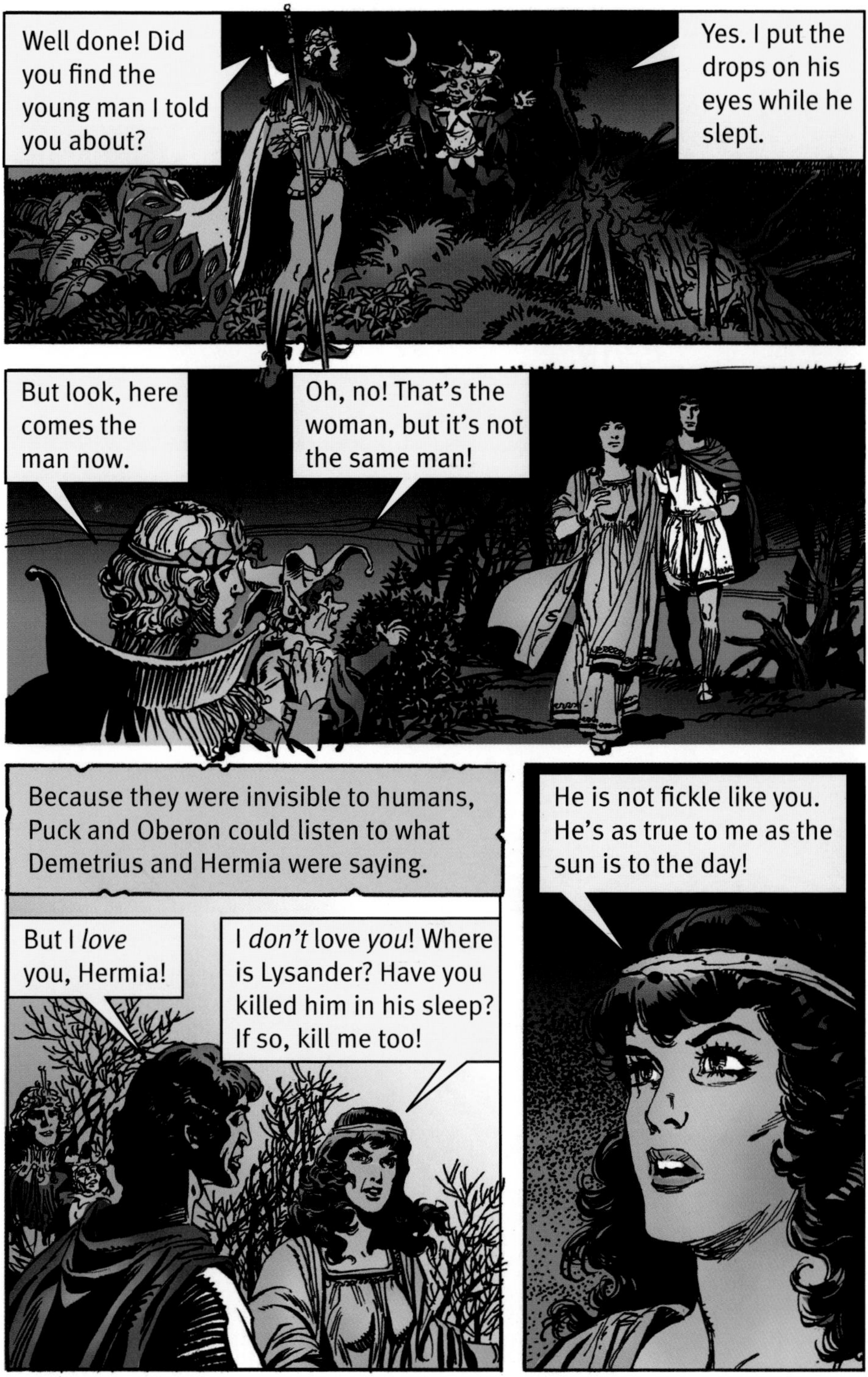
Well done! Did you find the young man I told you about?
Yes. I put the drops on his eyes while he slept.
But look, here comes the man now.
Oh, no! That's the woman, but it's not the same man!
Because they were invisible to humans, Puck and Oberon could listen to what Demetrius and Hermia were saying.
But I *love* you, Hermia!
I *don't* love *you*! Where is Lysander? Have you killed him in his sleep? If so, kill me too!
He is not fickle like you. He's as true to me as the sun is to the day!

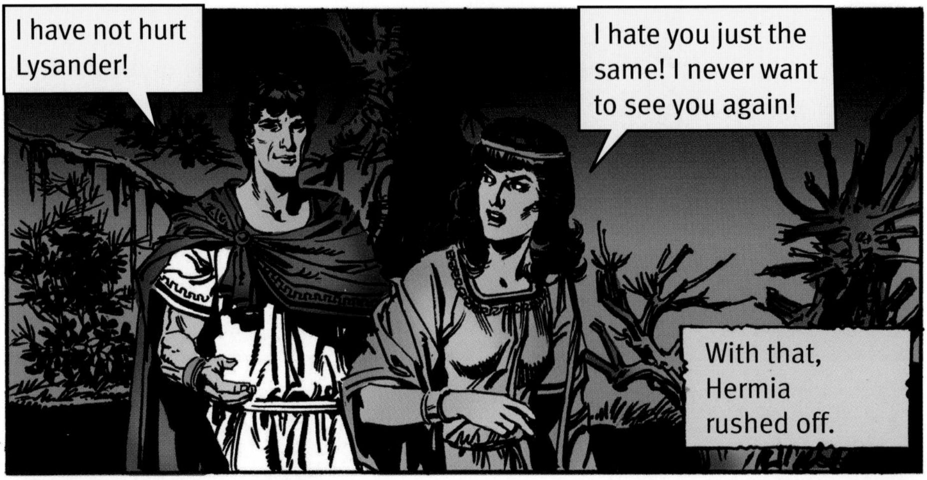
I have not hurt Lysander!
I hate you just the same! I never want to see you again!
With that, Hermia rushed off.

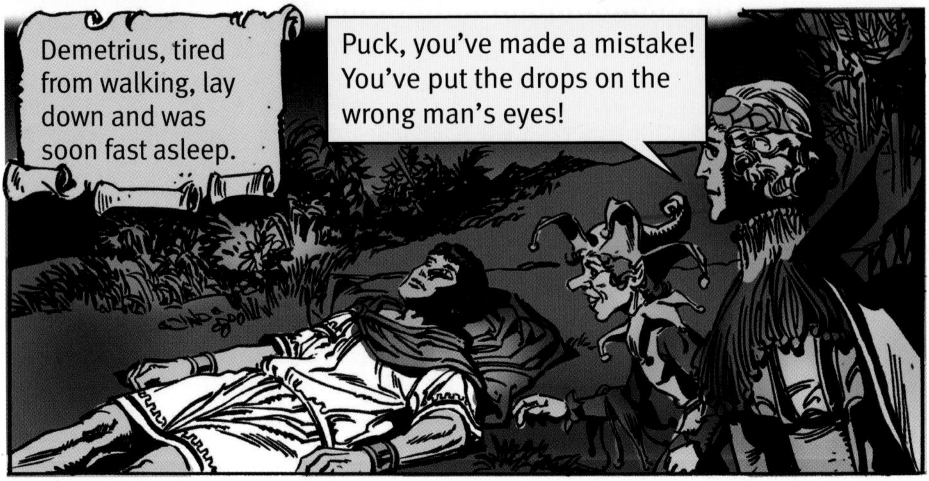
Demetrius, tired from walking, lay down and was soon fast asleep.
Puck, you've made a mistake! You've put the drops on the wrong man's eyes!

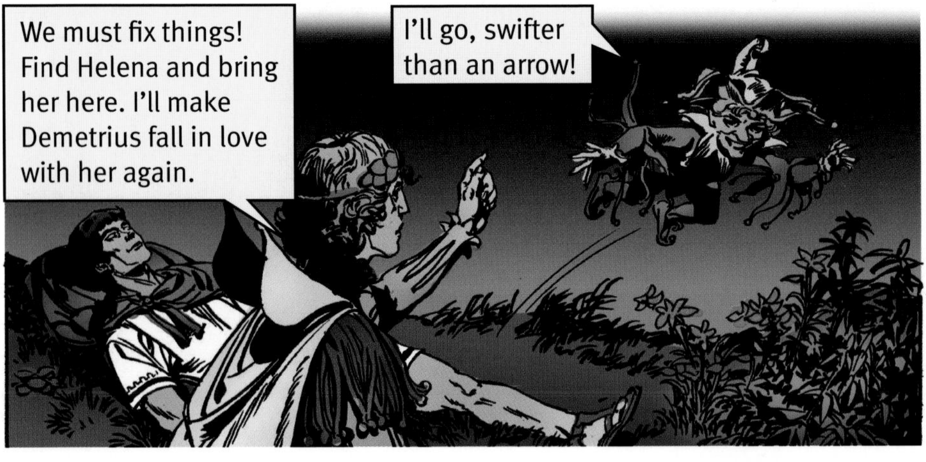
We must fix things! Find Helena and bring her here. I'll make Demetrius fall in love with her again.
I'll go, swifter than an arrow!

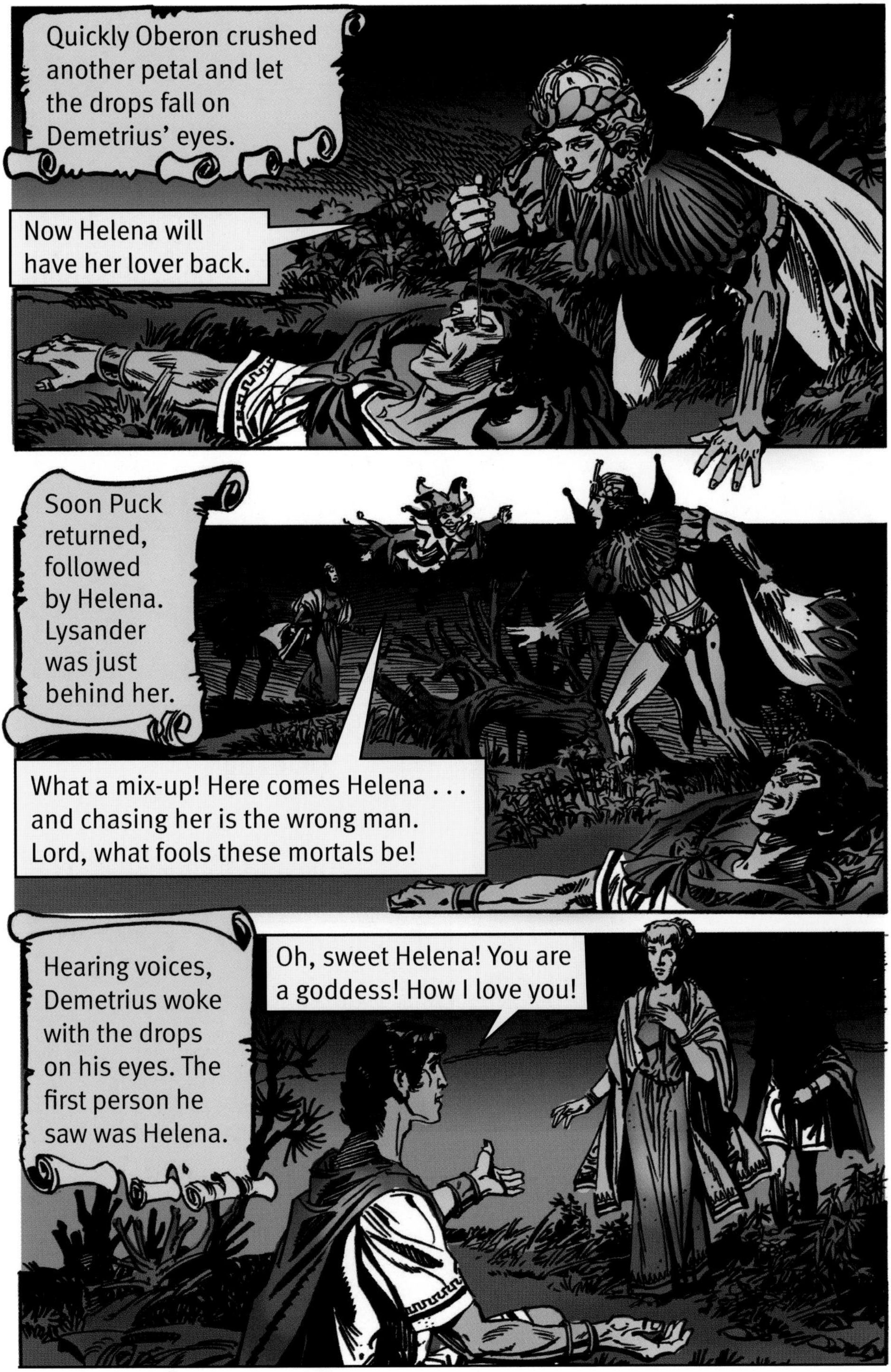
Quickly Oberon crushed another petal and let the drops fall on Demetrius' eyes.
Now Helena will have her lover back.
Soon Puck returned, followed by Helena. Lysander was just behind her.
What a mix-up! Here comes Helena . . . and chasing her is the wrong man. Lord, what fools these mortals be!
Hearing voices, Demetrius woke with the drops on his eyes. The first person he saw was Helena.
Oh, sweet Helena! You are a goddess! How I love you!

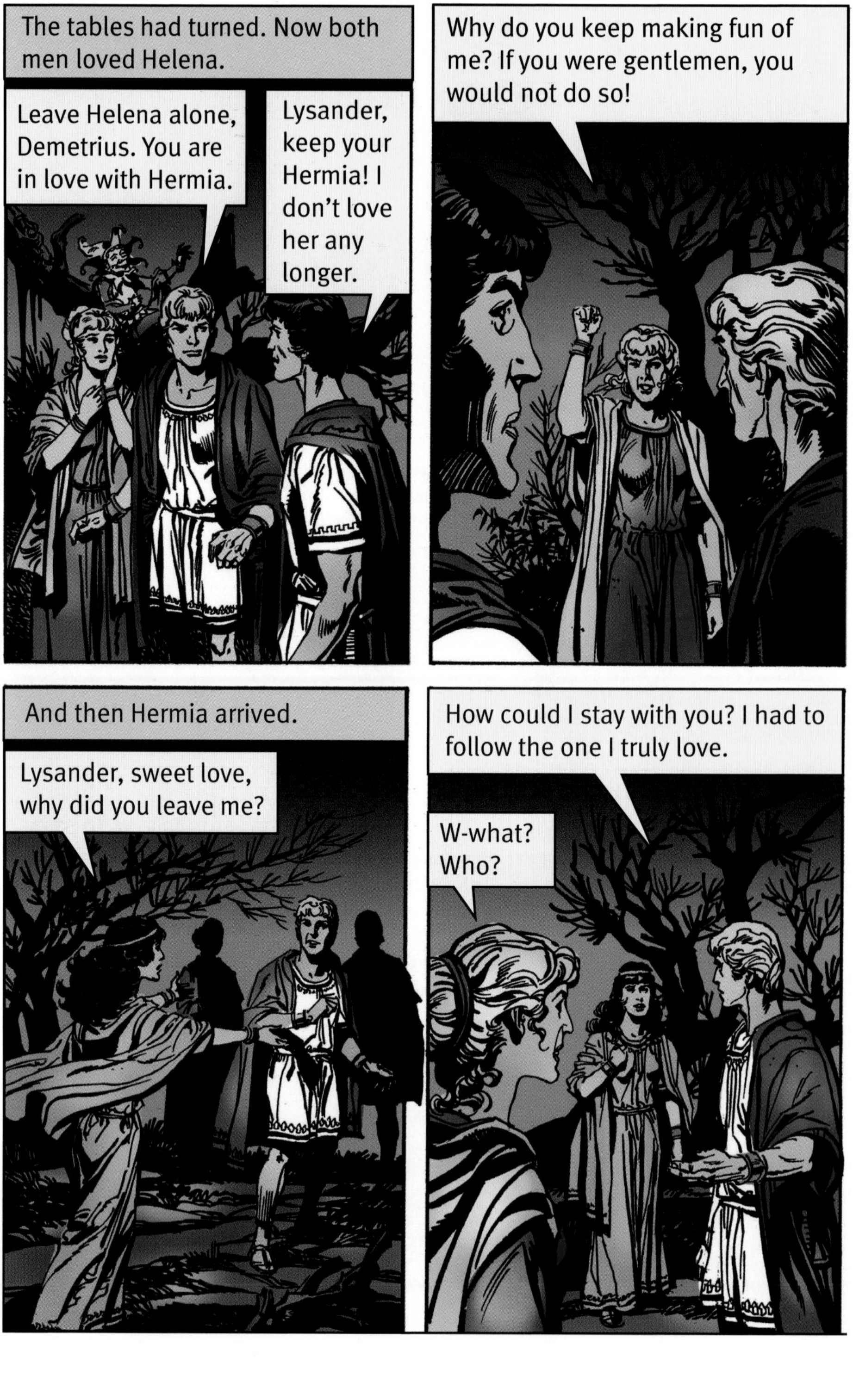
The tables had turned. Now both men loved Helena.
Leave Helena alone, Demetrius. You are in love with Hermia.
Lysander, keep your Hermia! I don't love her any longer.
Why do you keep making fun of me? If you were gentlemen, you would not do so!
And then Hermia arrived.
Lysander, sweet love, why did you leave me?
How could I stay with you? I had to follow the one I truly love.
W-what? Who?

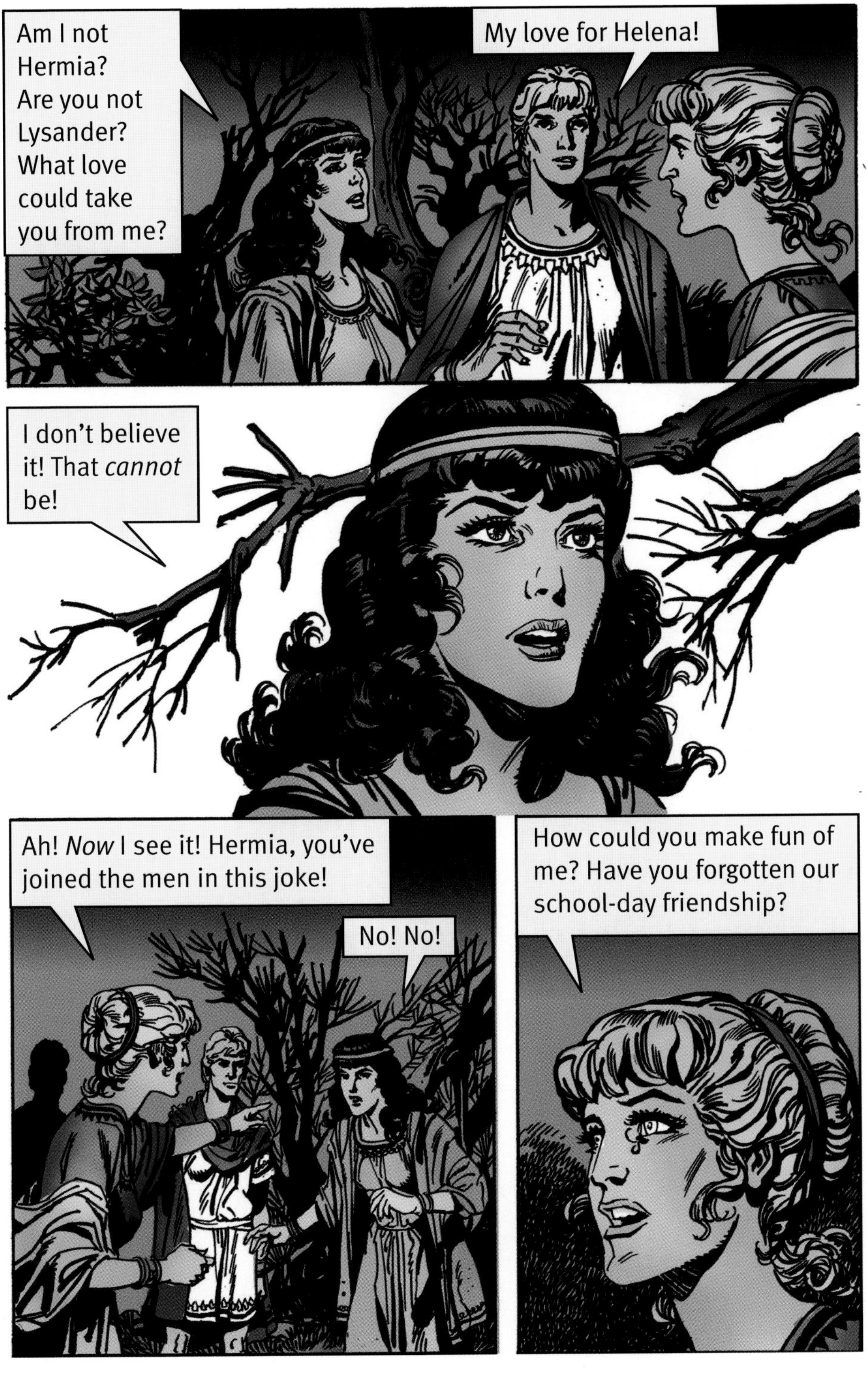
Am I not Hermia? Are you not Lysander? What love could take you from me?
My love for Helena!
I don't believe it! That *cannot* be!
Ah! *Now* I see it! Hermia, you've joined the men in this joke!
No! No!
How could you make fun of me? Have you forgotten our school-day friendship?

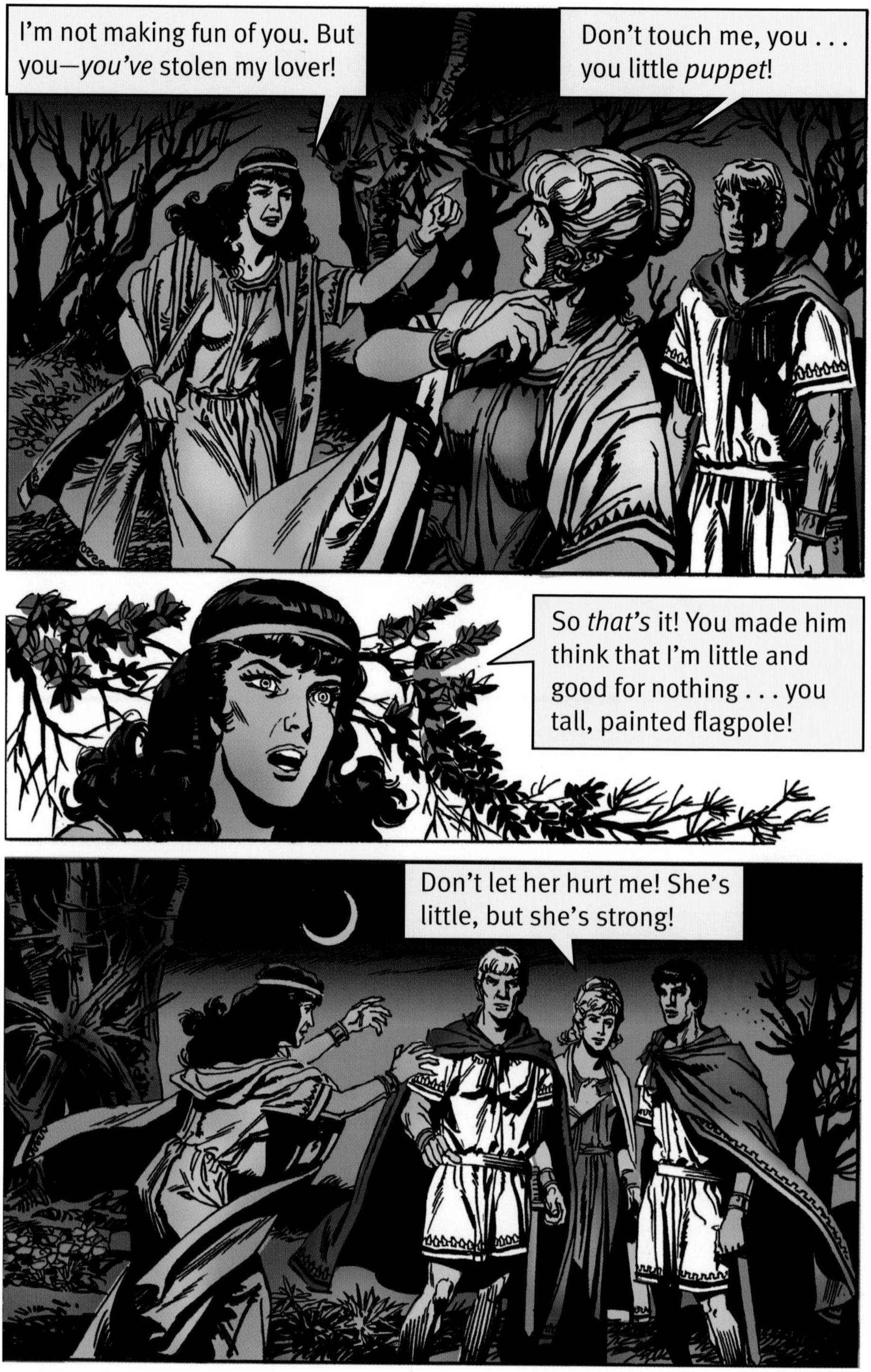
I'm not making fun of you. But you—*you've* stolen my lover!
Don't touch me, you . . . you little *puppet*!
So *that's* it! You made him think that I'm little and good for nothing . . . you tall, painted flagpole!
Don't let her hurt me! She's little, but she's strong!

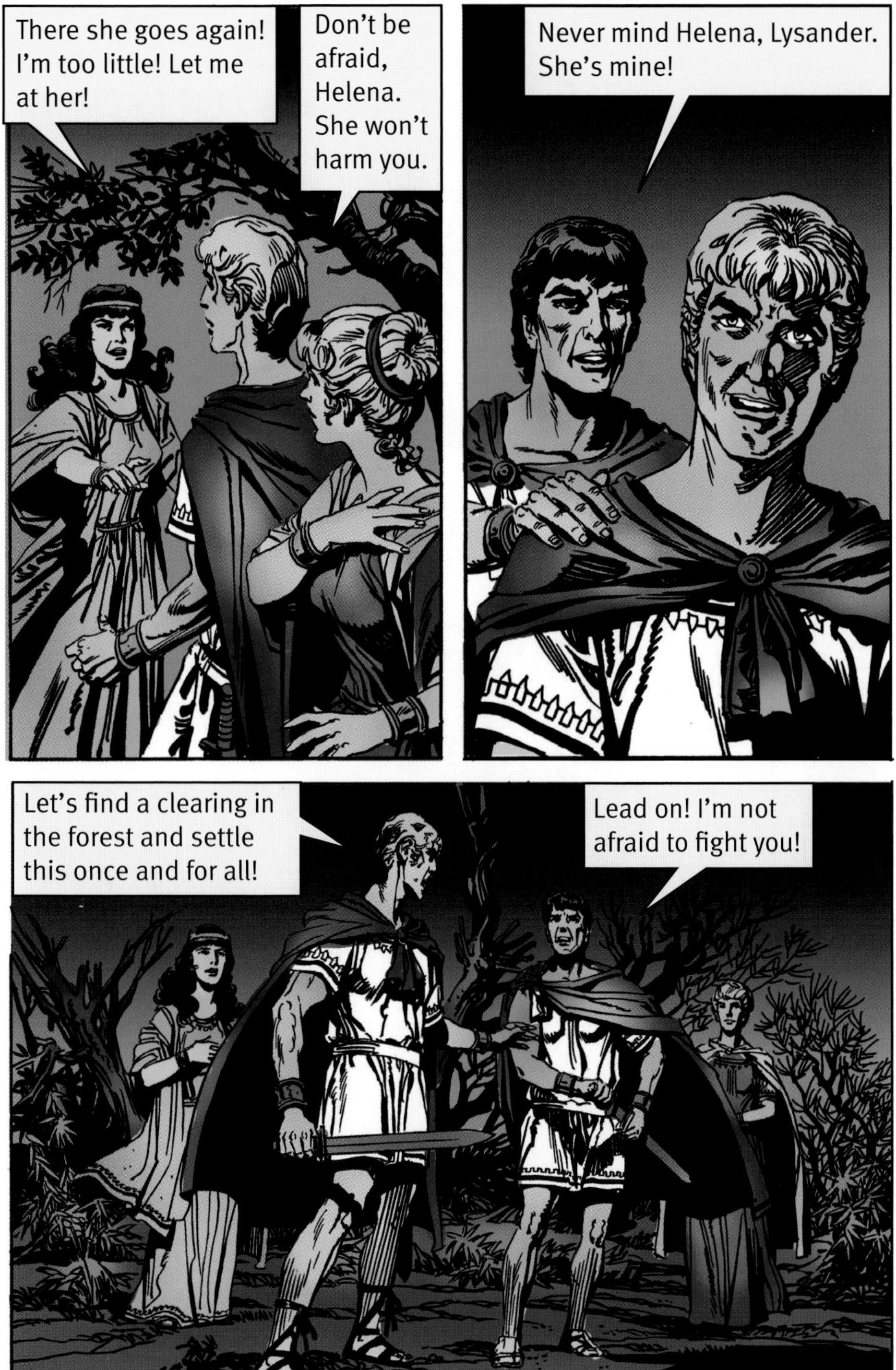
There she goes again! I'm too little! Let me at her!
Don't be afraid, Helena. She won't harm you.
Never mind Helena, Lysander. She's mine!
Let's find a clearing in the forest and settle this once and for all!
Lead on! I'm not afraid to fight you!

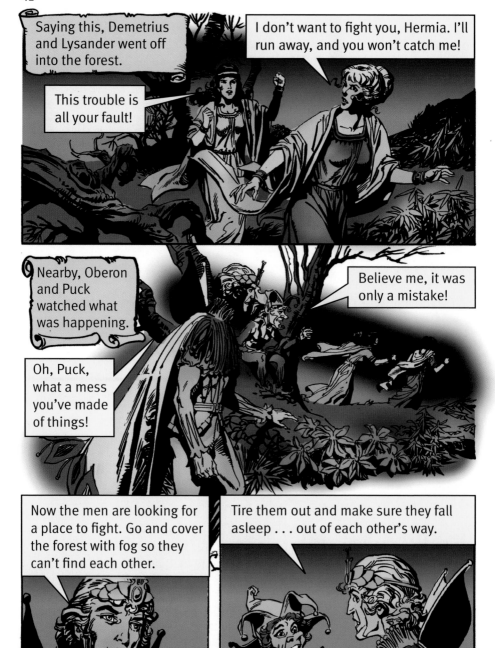

Saying this, Demetrius and Lysander went off into the forest.

This trouble is all your fault!

I don't want to fight you, Hermia. I'll run away, and you won't catch me!

Nearby, Oberon and Puck watched what was happening.

Believe me, it was only a mistake!

Oh, Puck, what a mess you've made of things!

Now the men are looking for a place to fight. Go and cover the forest with fog so they can't find each other.

Tire them out and make sure they fall asleep . . . out of each other's way.

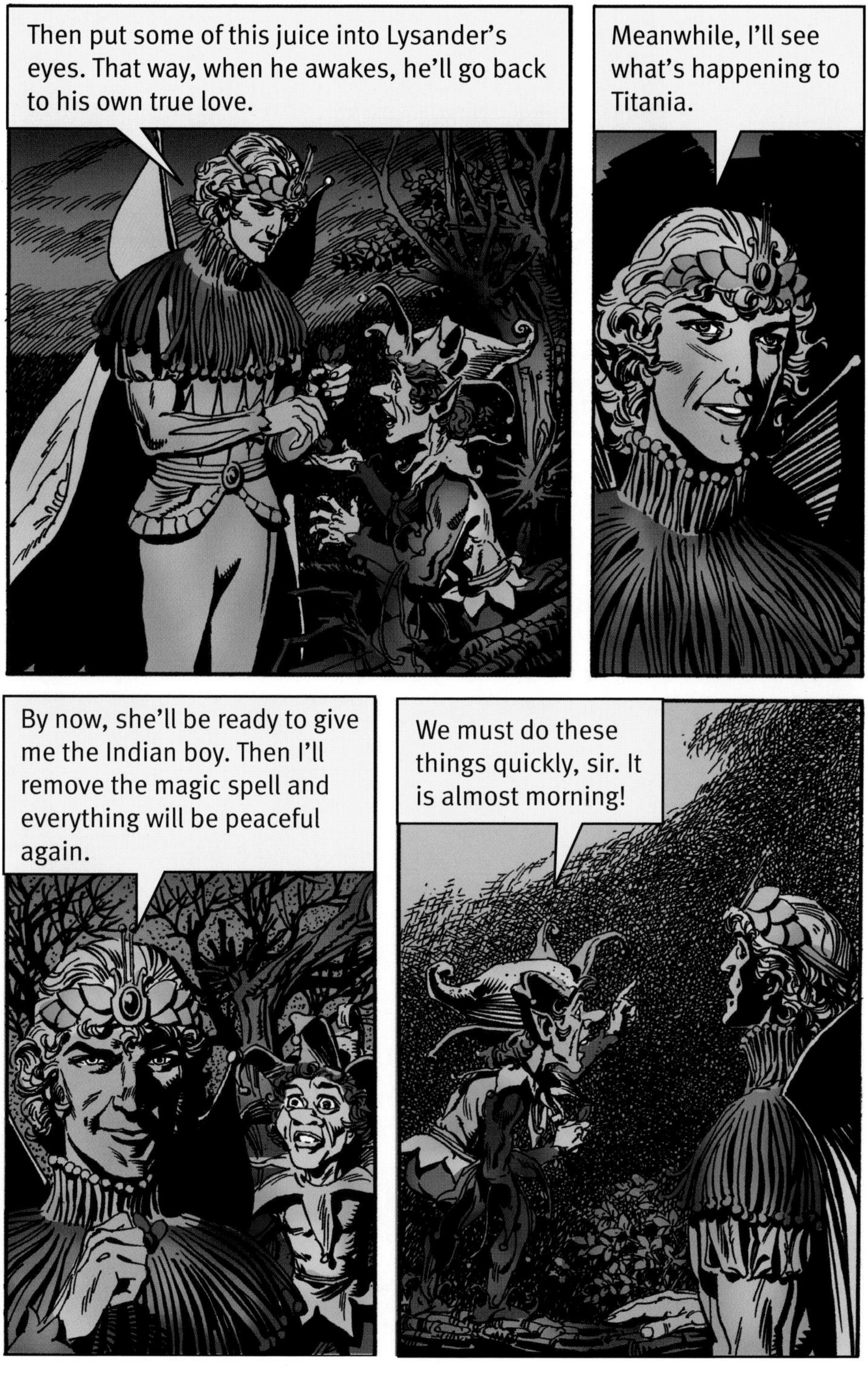
Then put some of this juice into Lysander's eyes. That way, when he awakes, he'll go back to his own true love.
Meanwhile, I'll see what's happening to Titania.
By now, she'll be ready to give me the Indian boy. Then I'll remove the magic spell and everything will be peaceful again.
We must do these things quickly, sir. It is almost morning!

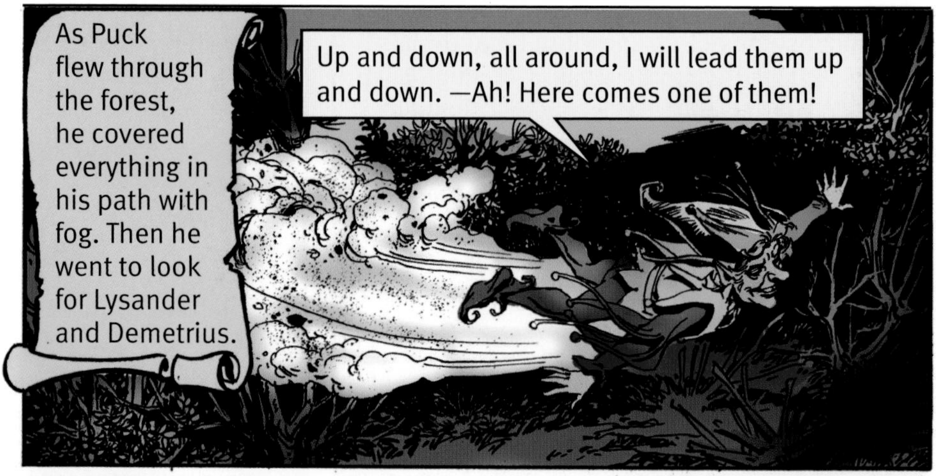
As Puck flew through the forest, he covered everything in his path with fog. Then he went to look for Lysander and Demetrius.
Up and down, all around, I will lead them up and down. —Ah! Here comes one of them!

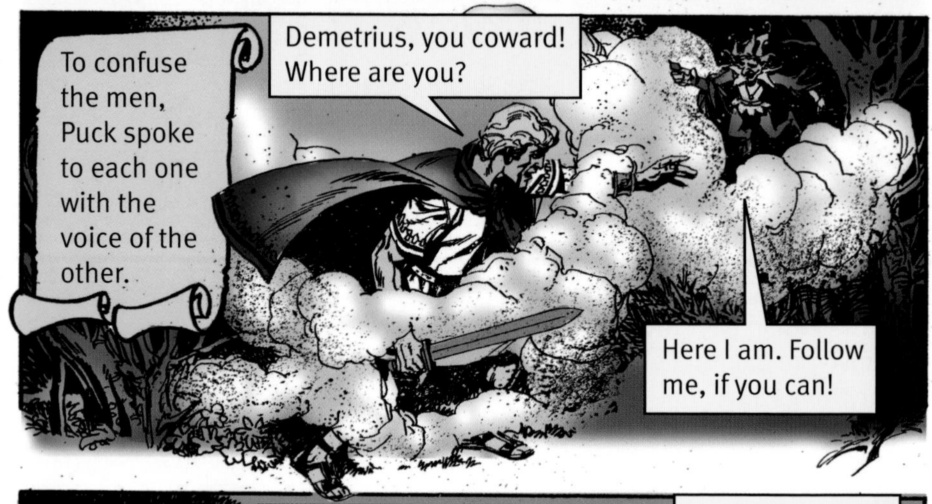
To confuse the men, Puck spoke to each one with the voice of the other.
Demetrius, you coward! Where are you?
Here I am. Follow me, if you can!

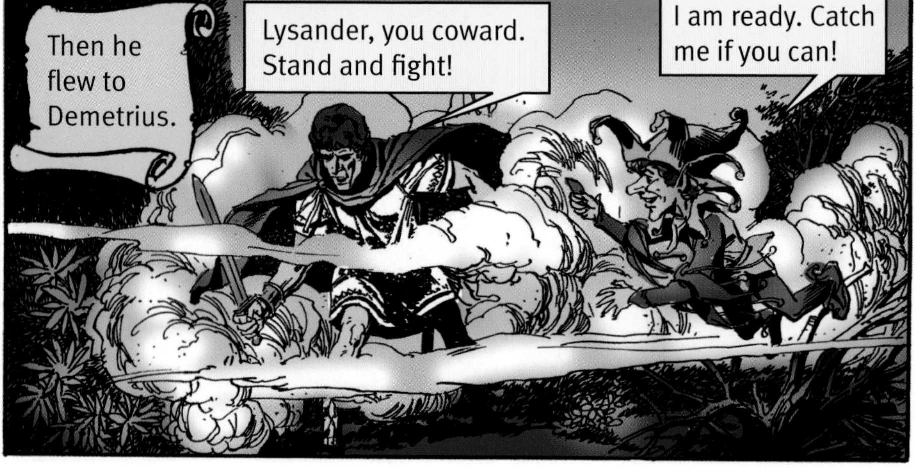
Then he flew to Demetrius.
Lysander, you coward. Stand and fight!
I am ready. Catch me if you can!

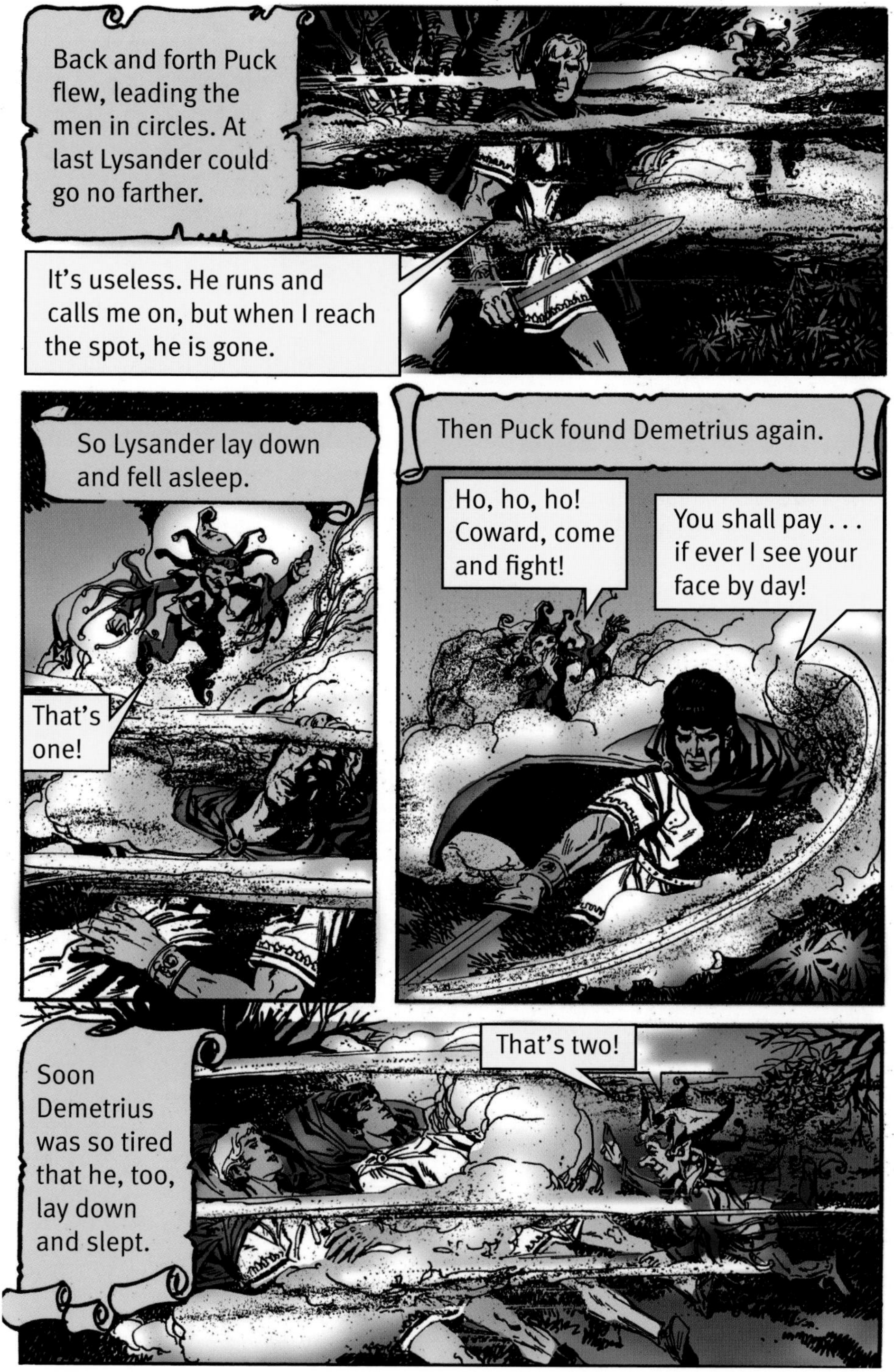
Back and forth Puck flew, leading the men in circles. At last Lysander could go no farther.
It's useless. He runs and calls me on, but when I reach the spot, he is gone.
So Lysander lay down and fell asleep.
That's one!
Then Puck found Demetrius again.
Ho, ho, ho! Coward, come and fight!
You shall pay . . . if ever I see your face by day!
Soon Demetrius was so tired that he, too, lay down and slept.
That's two!

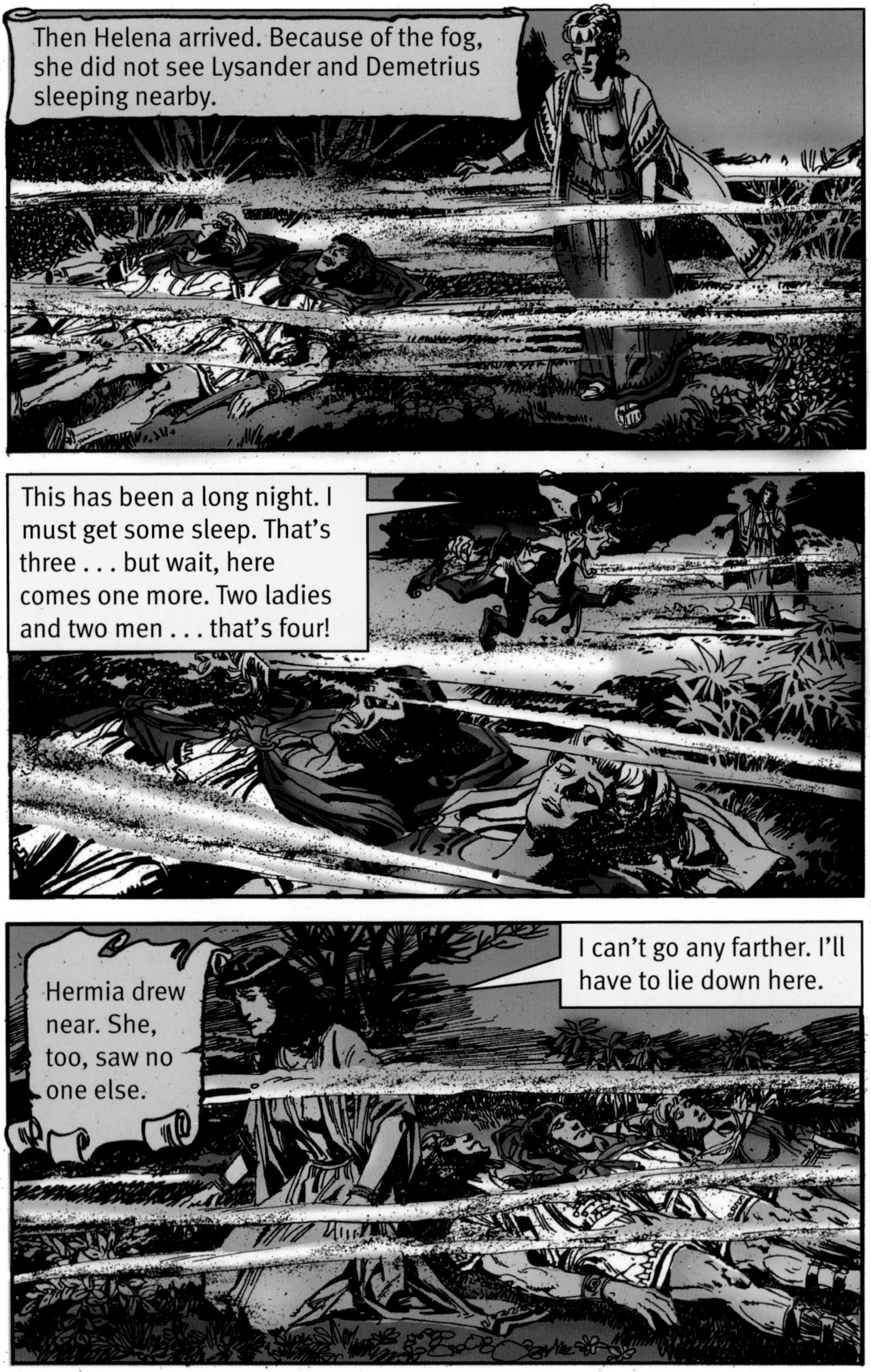
Then Helena arrived. Because of the fog, she did not see Lysander and Demetrius sleeping nearby.
This has been a long night. I must get some sleep. That's three . . . but wait, here comes one more. Two ladies and two men . . . that's four!
Hermia drew near. She, too, saw no one else.
I can't go any farther. I'll have to lie down here.

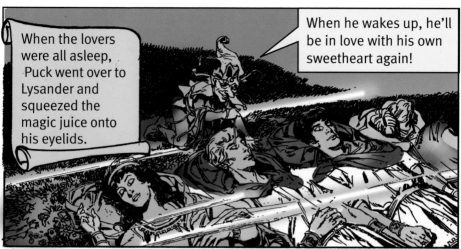

When the lovers were all asleep, Puck went over to Lysander and squeezed the magic juice onto his eyelids.

When he wakes up, he'll be in love with his own sweetheart again!

Then Puck went to Oberon, who got his wish. Queen Titania had given him the Indian boy. But she was still under the magic spell.

Welcome, good Puck! The night is almost over, and soon it will seem that all that has happened was only a dream!

Then he freed Queen Titania from the magic of Cupid's flower.

Now wake, my sweet queen, and be your true self again!

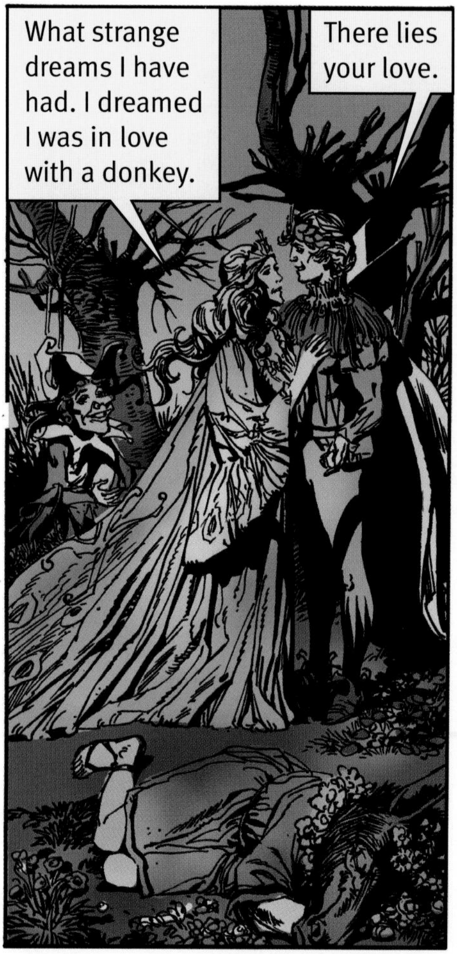
What strange dreams I have had. I dreamed I was in love with a donkey.
There lies your love.

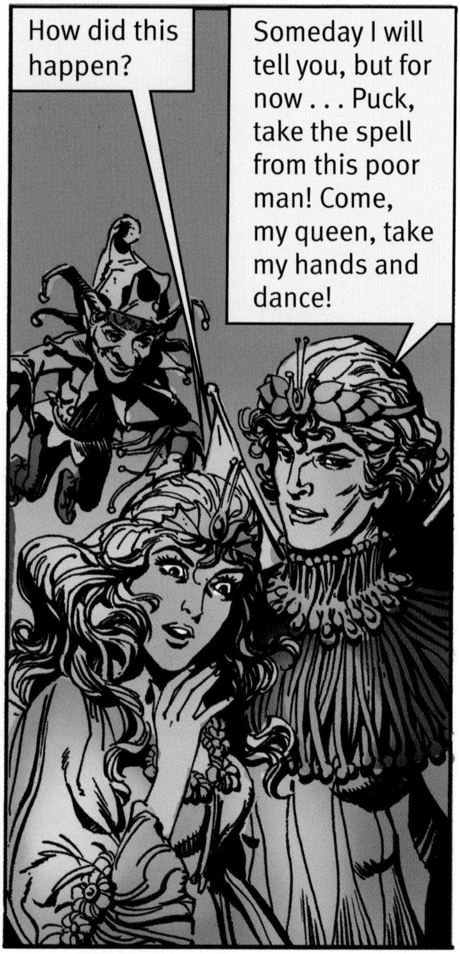
How did this happen?
Someday I will tell you, but for now . . . Puck, take the spell from this poor man! Come, my queen, take my hands and dance!

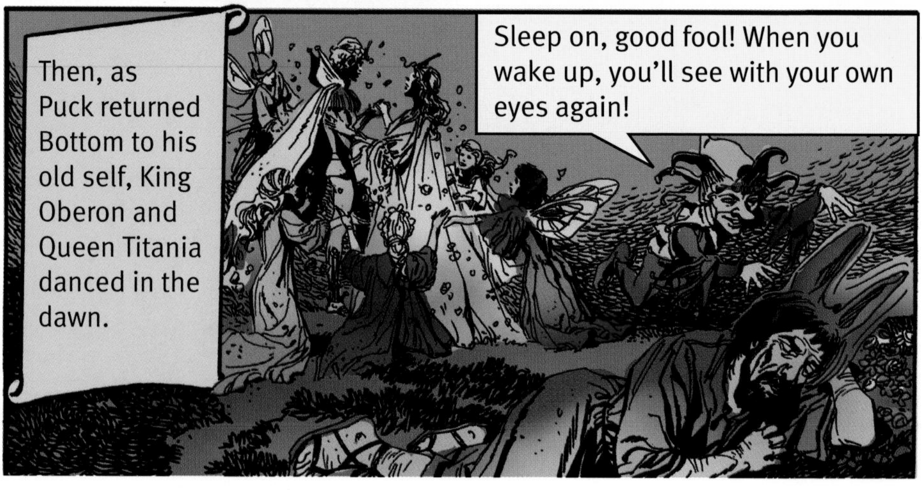
Then, as Puck returned Bottom to his old self, King Oberon and Queen Titania danced in the dawn.
Sleep on, good fool! When you wake up, you'll see with your own eyes again!

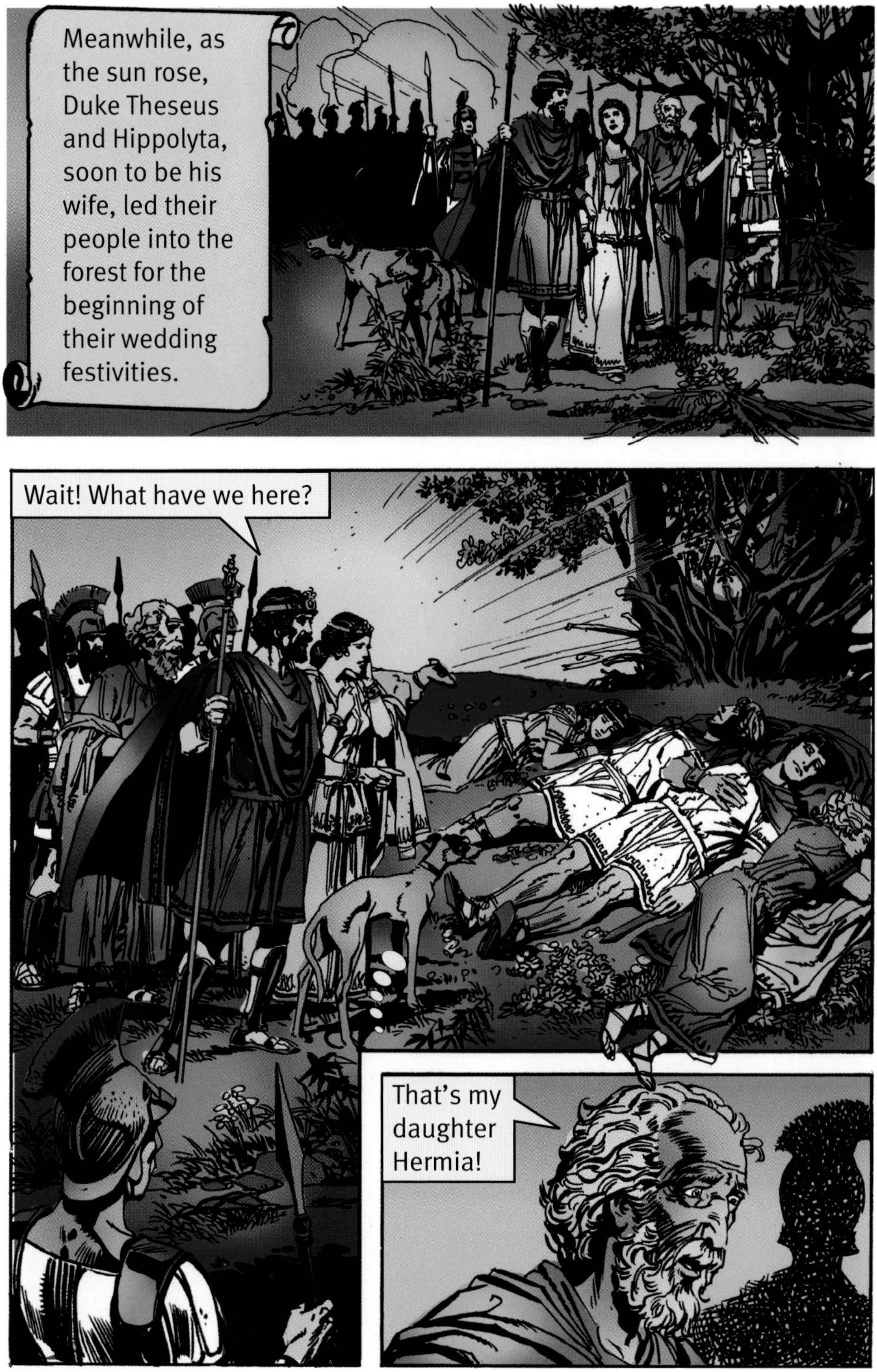
Meanwhile, as the sun rose, Duke Theseus and Hippolyta, soon to be his wife, led their people into the forest for the beginning of their wedding festivities.
Wait! What have we here?
That's my daughter Hermia!

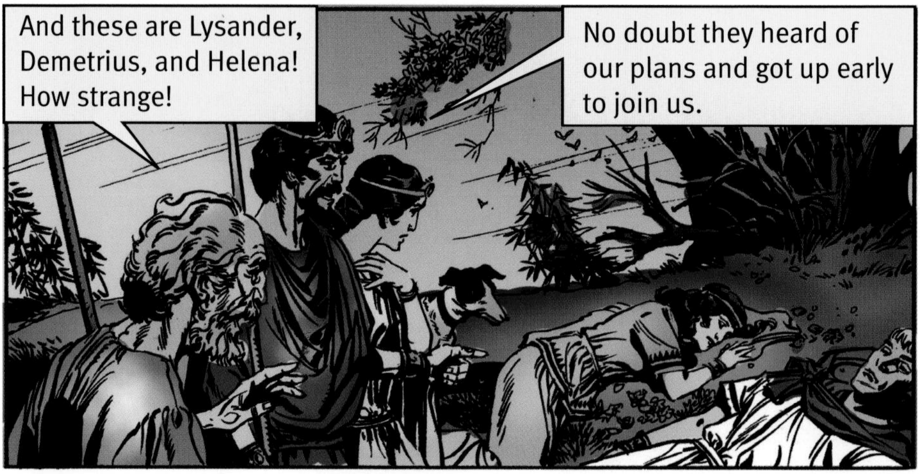
And these are Lysander, Demetrius, and Helena! How strange!
No doubt they heard of our plans and got up early to join us.

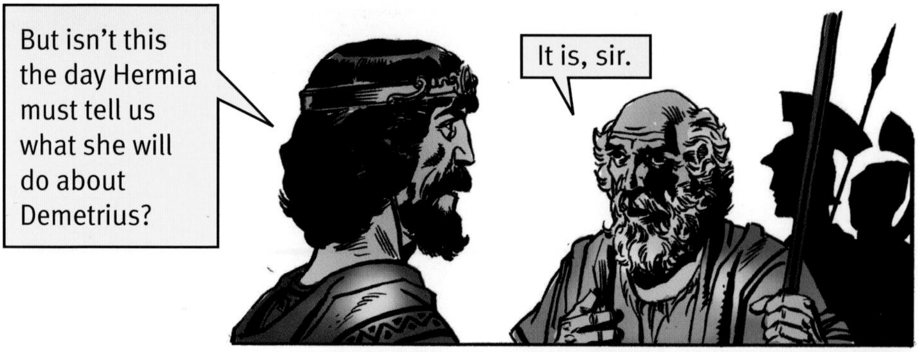
But isn't this the day Hermia must tell us what she will do about Demetrius?
It is, sir.

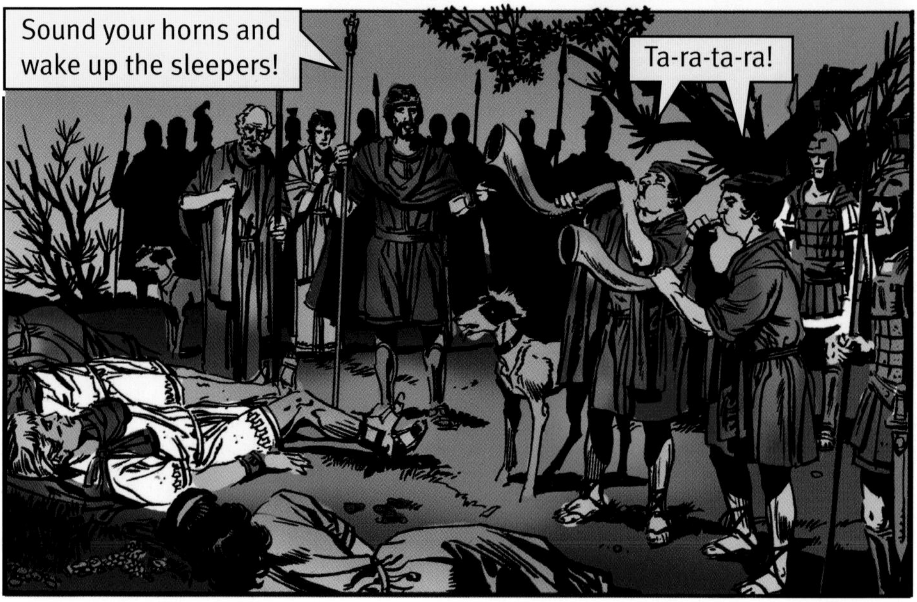
Sound your horns and wake up the sleepers!
Ta-ra-ta-ra!

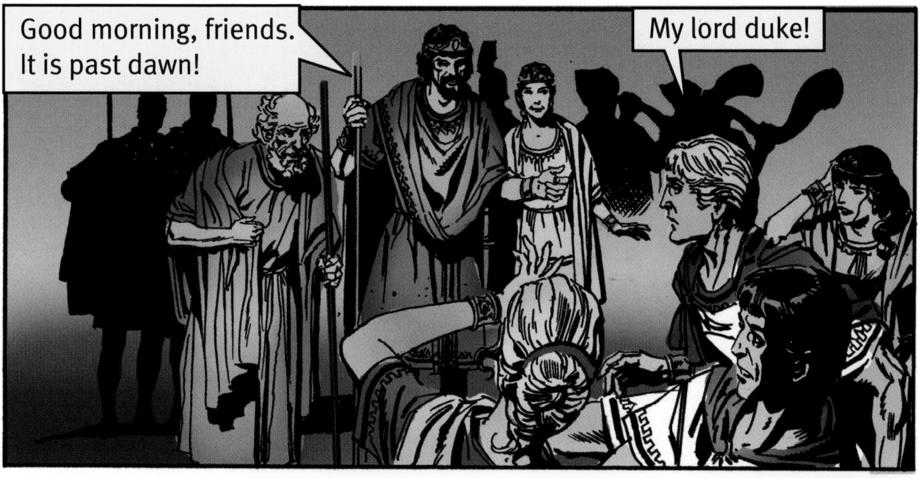
Good morning, friends. It is past dawn!
My lord duke!

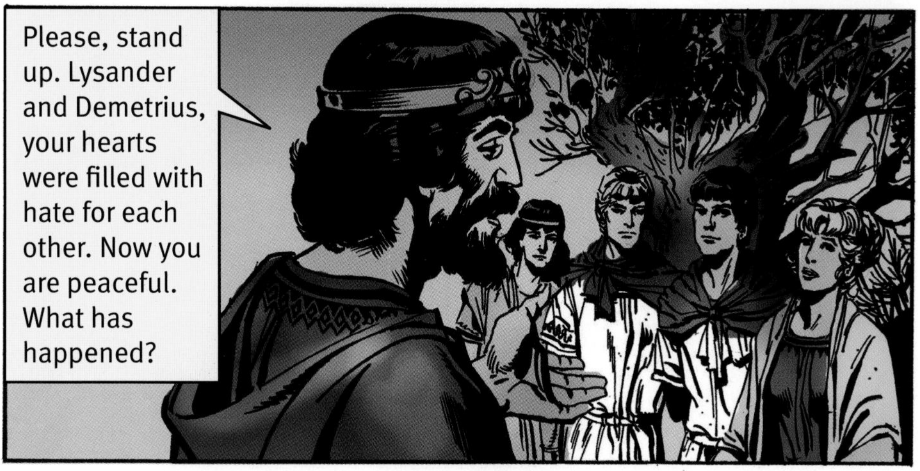
Please, stand up. Lysander and Demetrius, your hearts were filled with hate for each other. Now you are peaceful. What has happened?

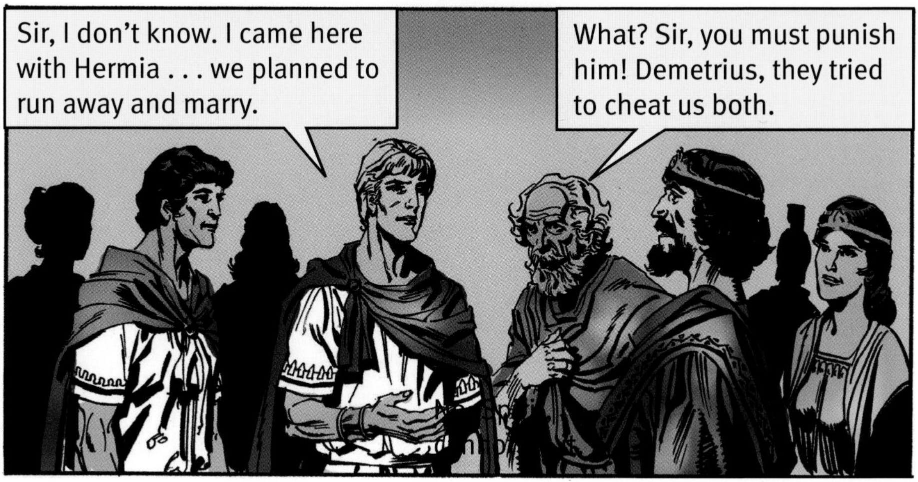
Sir, I don't know. I came here with Hermia . . . we planned to run away and marry.
What? Sir, you must punish him! Demetrius, they tried to cheat us both.

Sir, Helena told me of their plan and I followed them here in anger.

But by some unknown power, my love for Hermia has melted away. Meanwhile, my love for Helena has returned stronger than ever!

Now I wish the greatest happiness for Hermia and Lysander! And I want to marry Helena!

This is good fortune! I invite both couples to come to the temple. They will be married at the same time I marry Hippolyta!

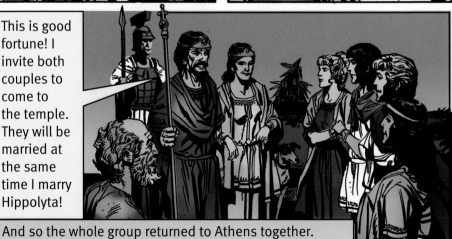

And so the whole group returned to Athens together.

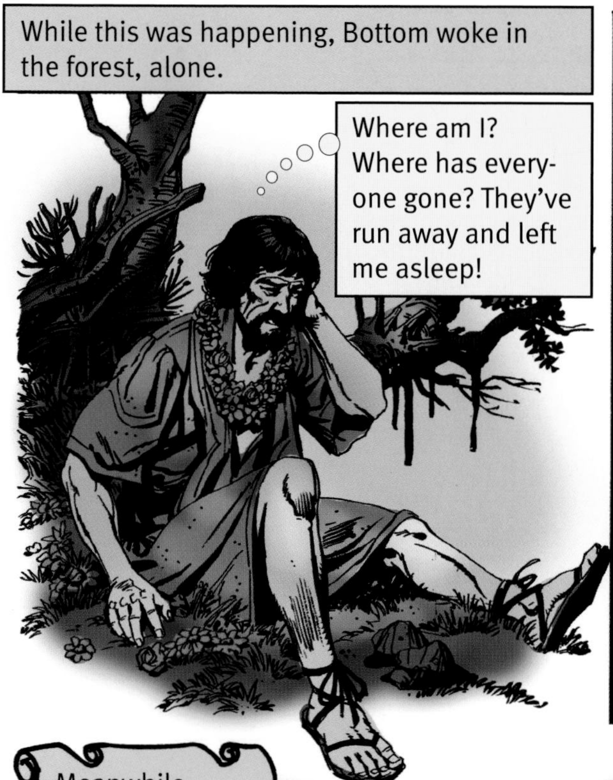
While this was happening, Bottom woke in the forest, alone.
Where am I? Where has every-one gone? They've run away and left me asleep!

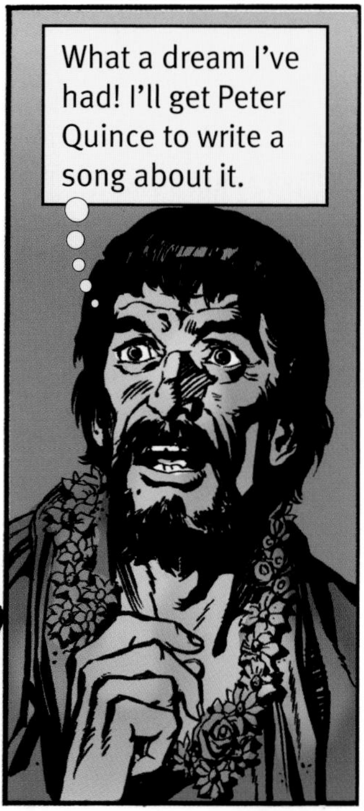
What a dream I've had! I'll get Peter Quince to write a song about it.

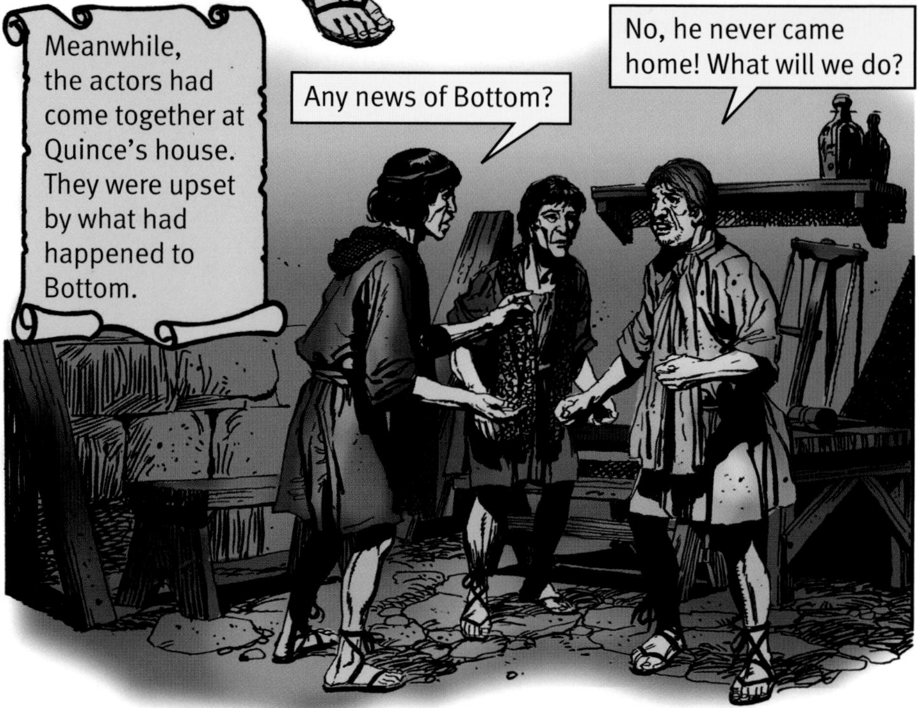
Meanwhile, the actors had come together at Quince's house. They were upset by what had happened to Bottom.
Any news of Bottom?
No, he never came home! What will we do?

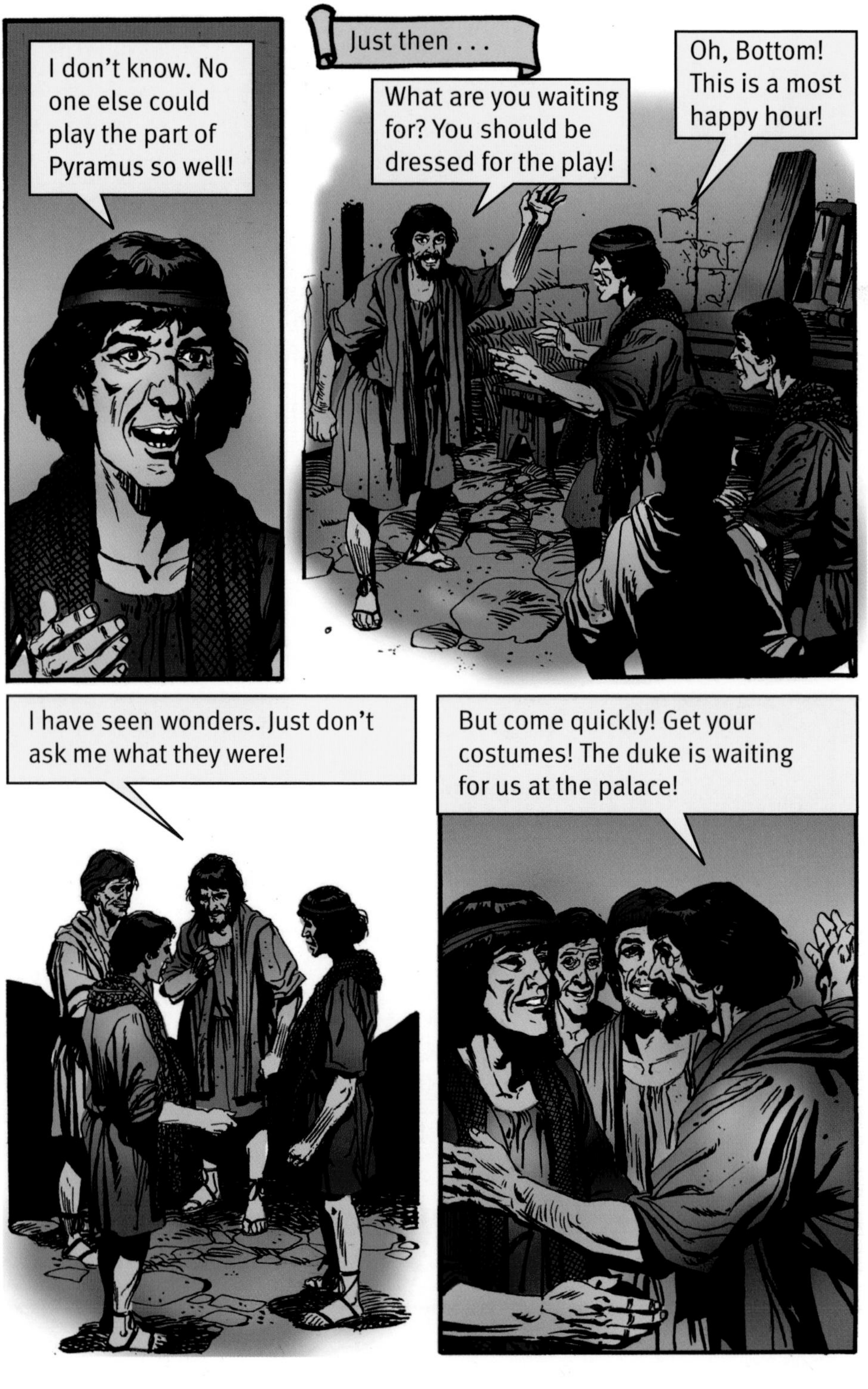
I don't know. No one else could play the part of Pyramus so well!
Just then . . .
What are you waiting for? You should be dressed for the play!
Oh, Bottom! This is a most happy hour!
I have seen wonders. Just don't ask me what they were!
But come quickly! Get your costumes! The duke is waiting for us at the palace!

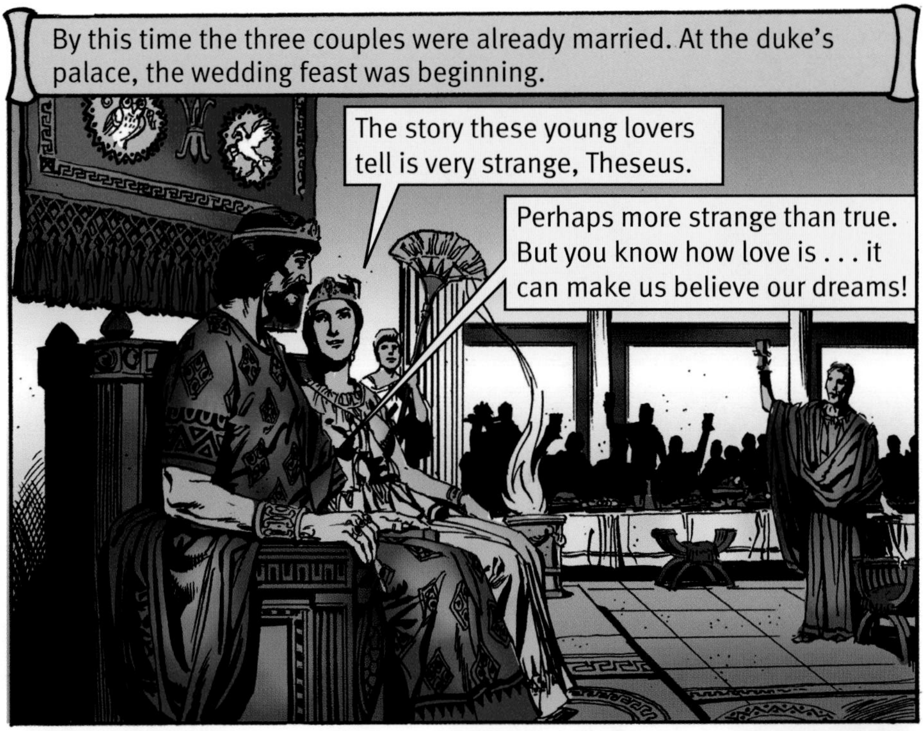
By this time the three couples were already married. At the duke's palace, the wedding feast was beginning.
The story these young lovers tell is very strange, Theseus.
Perhaps more strange than true. But you know how love is . . . it can make us believe our dreams!

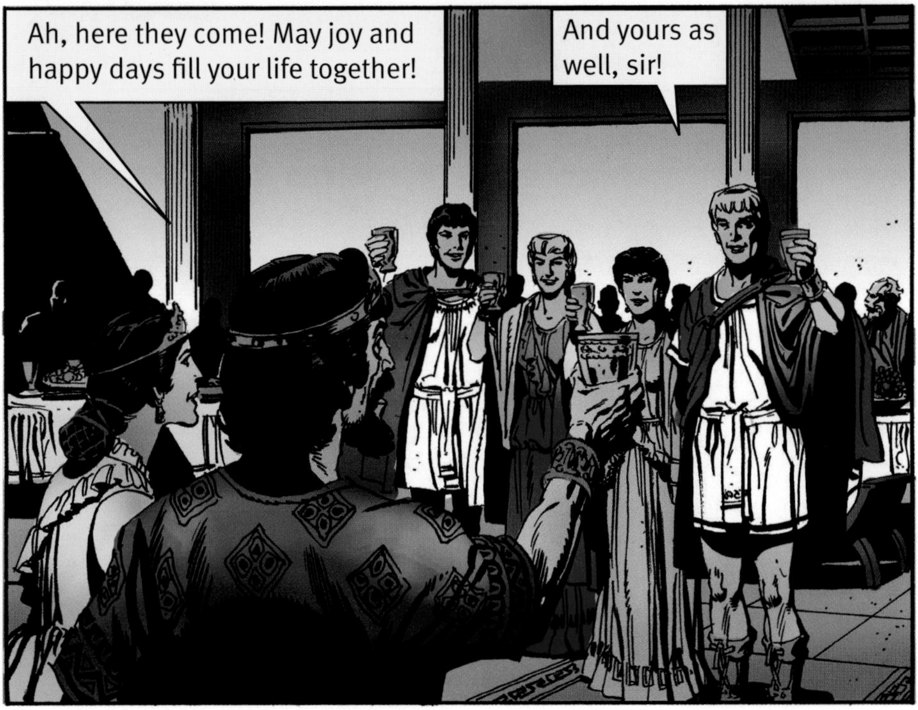
Ah, here they come! May joy and happy days fill your life together!
And yours as well, sir!

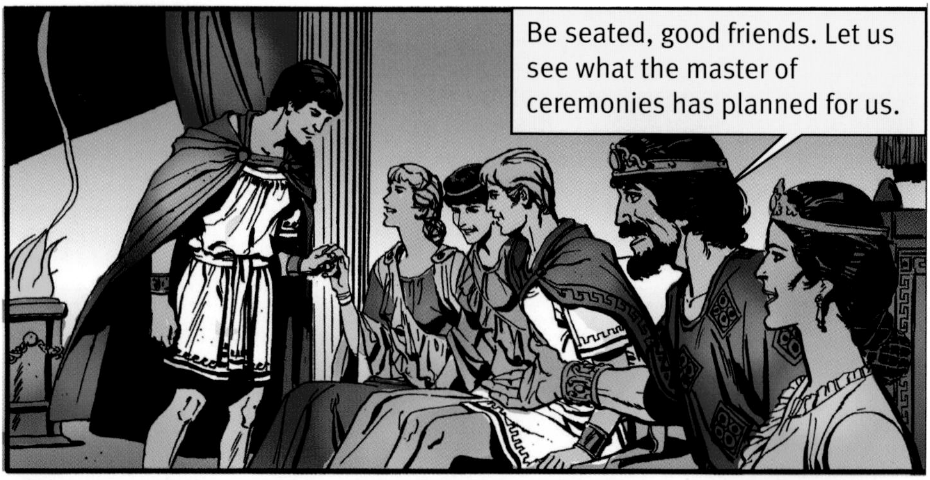
Be seated, good friends. Let us see what the master of ceremonies has planned for us.

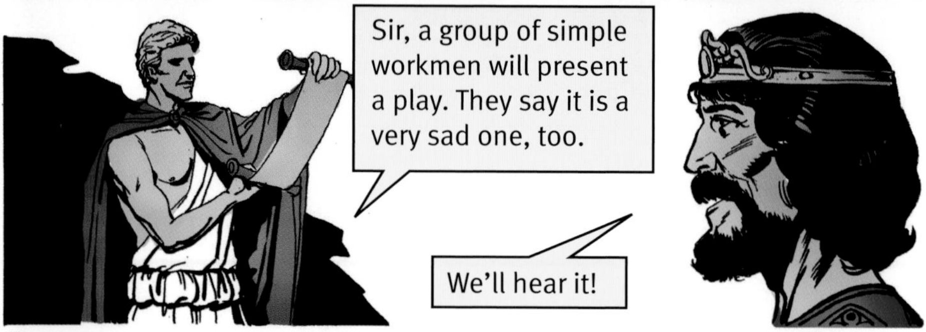
Sir, a group of simple workmen will present a play. They say it is a very sad one, too.
We'll hear it!

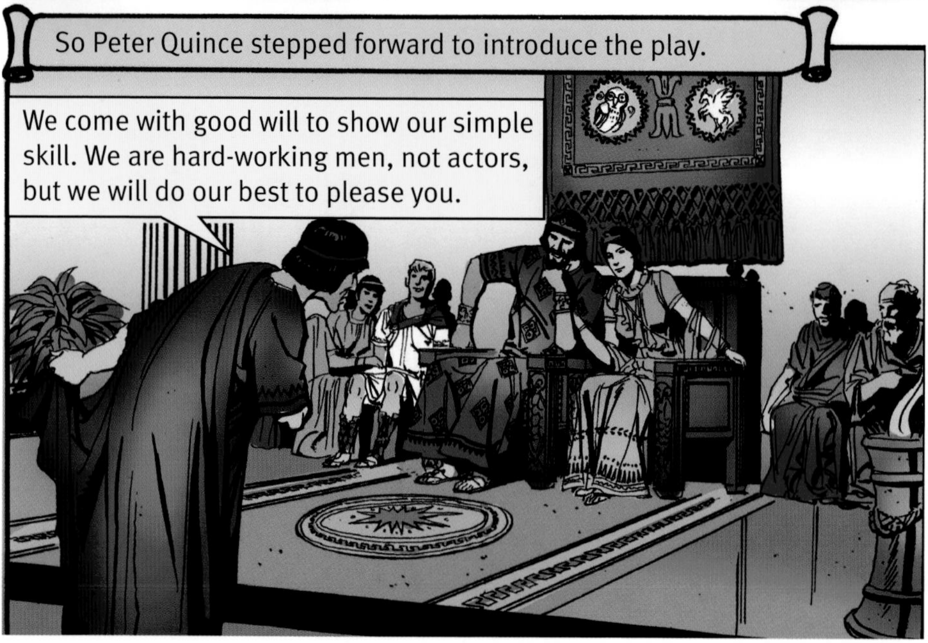
So Peter Quince stepped forward to introduce the play.
We come with good will to show our simple skill. We are hard-working men, not actors, but we will do our best to please you.

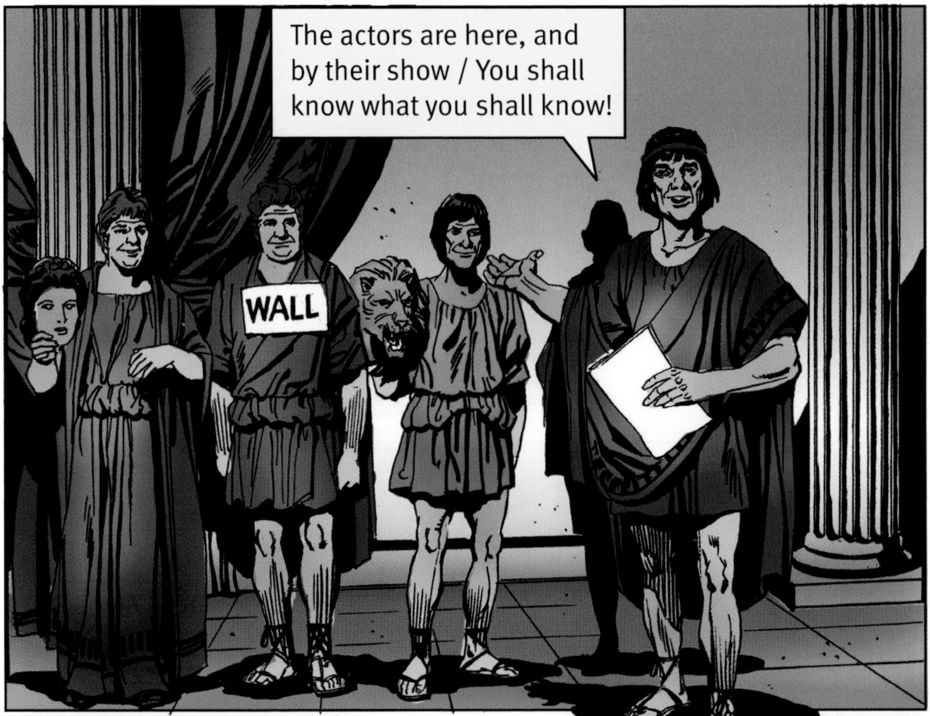
The actors are here, and by their show / You shall know what you shall know!
WALL

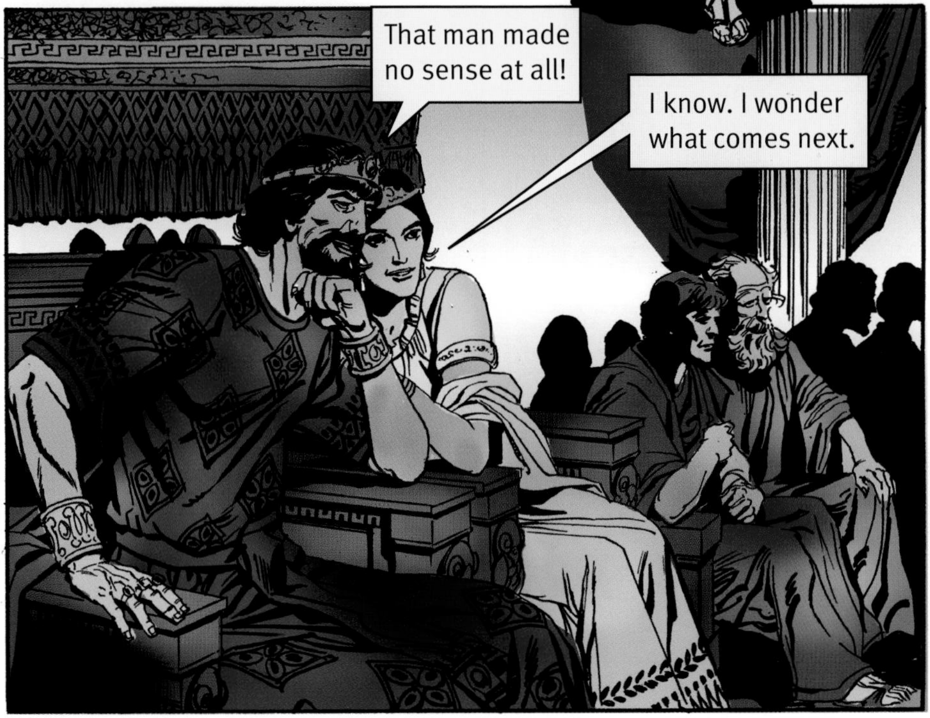
That man made no sense at all!
I know. I wonder what comes next.

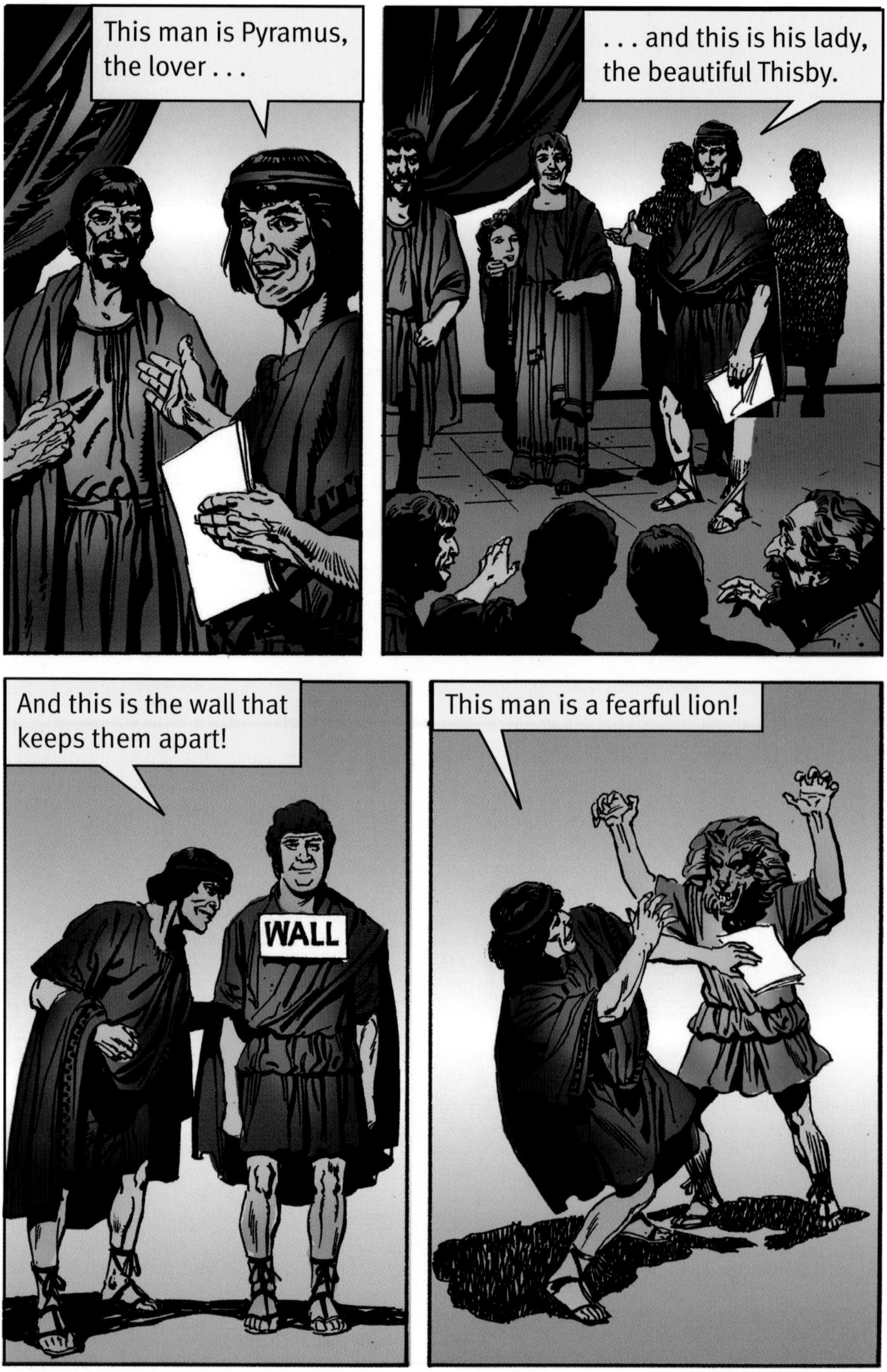
This man is Pyramus, the lover . . .
. . . and this is his lady, the beautiful Thisby.
And this is the wall that keeps them apart!
WALL
This man is a fearful lion!

And so the play began.

Then Pyramus entered.

As you know, I am a wall. I have a handy chink through which the lovers whisper.

I hope my Thisby doesn't forget her promise to meet me here.

At this, Thisby entered from the other side of the wall.

Oh, wall, why do you keep me from my love?

I see a voice! I hear my Thisby's face!

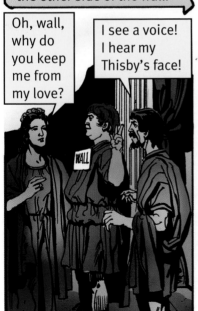

Thisby!

My love!

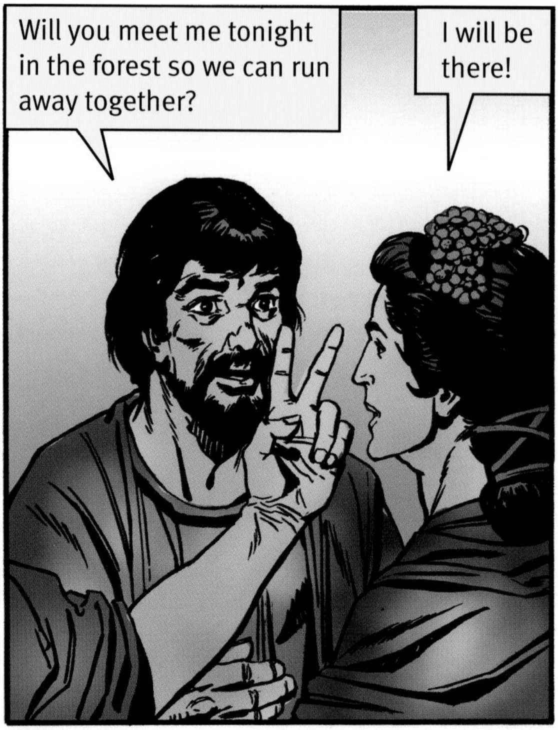
Will you meet me tonight in the forest so we can run away together?
I will be there!

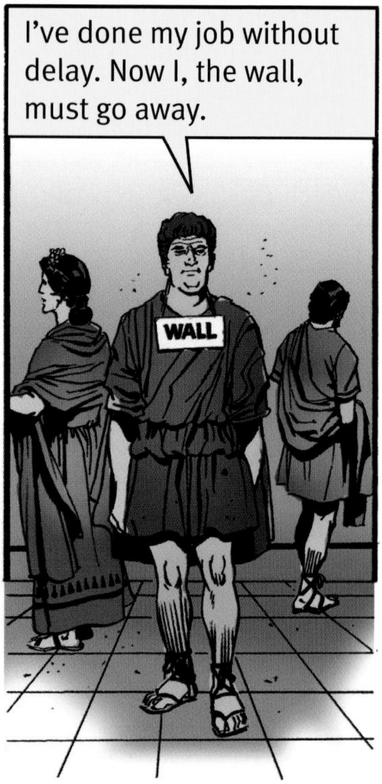
I've done my job without delay. Now I, the wall, must go away.
WALL

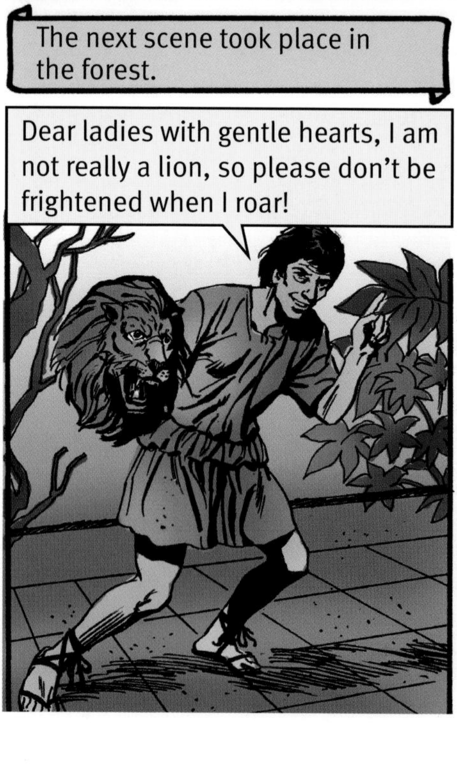
The next scene took place in the forest.
Dear ladies with gentle hearts, I am not really a lion, so please don't be frightened when I roar!

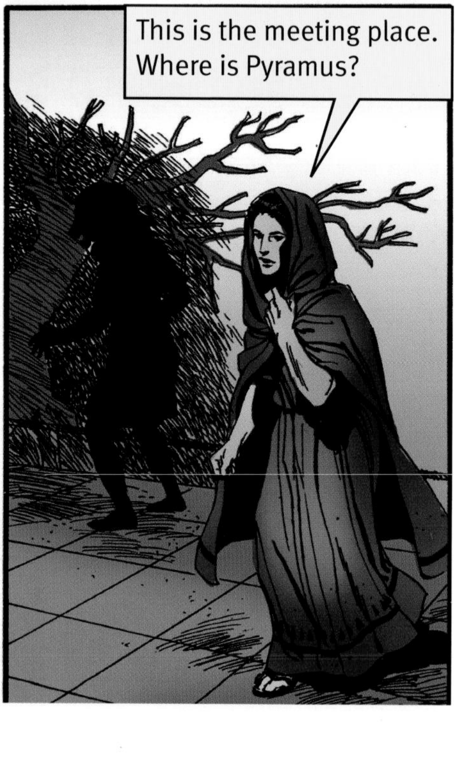
This is the meeting place. Where is Pyramus?

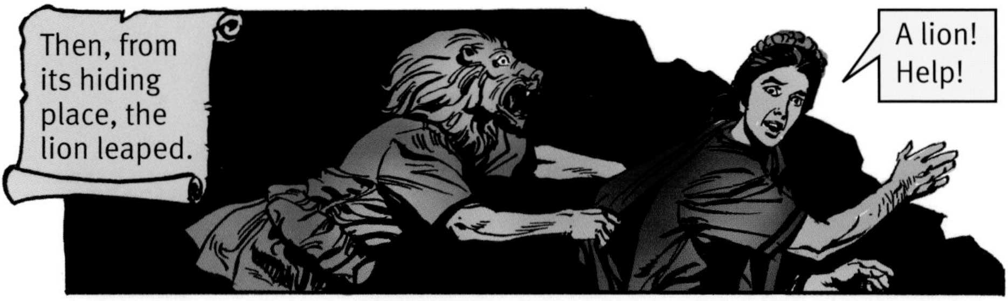
Then, from its hiding place, the lion leaped.
A lion! Help!

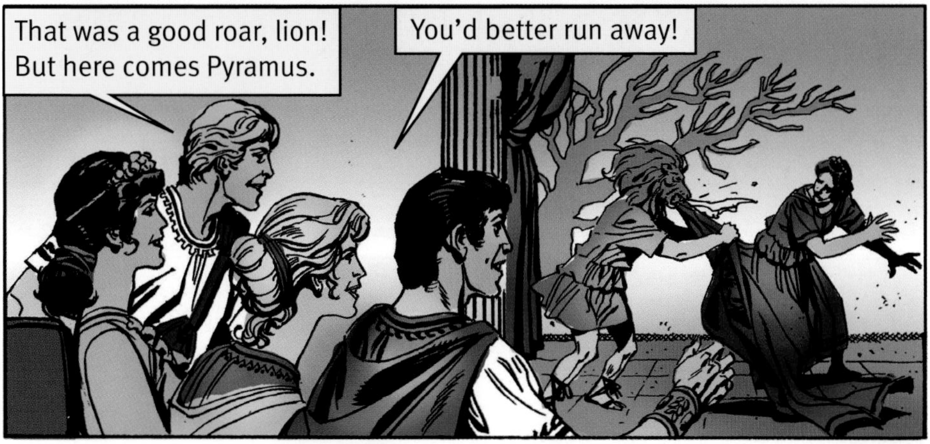
That was a good roar, lion! But here comes Pyramus.
You'd better run away!

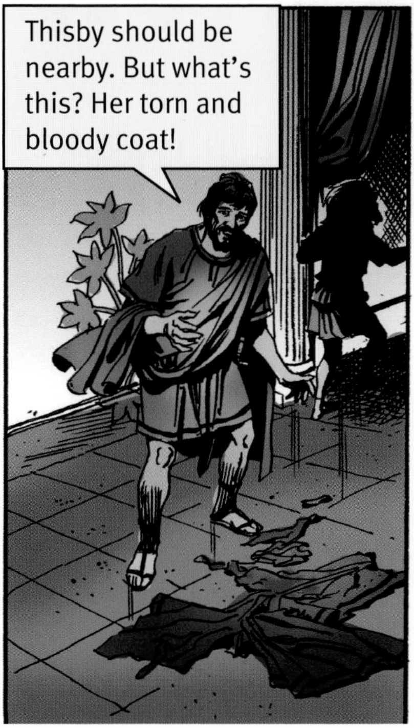
Thisby should be nearby. But what's this? Her torn and bloody coat!

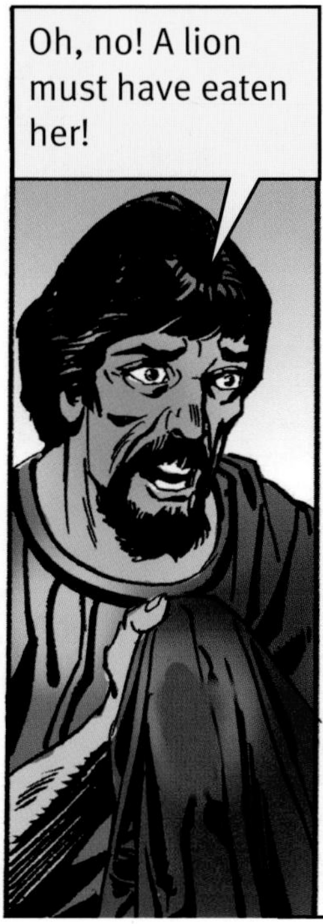
Oh, no! A lion must have eaten her!

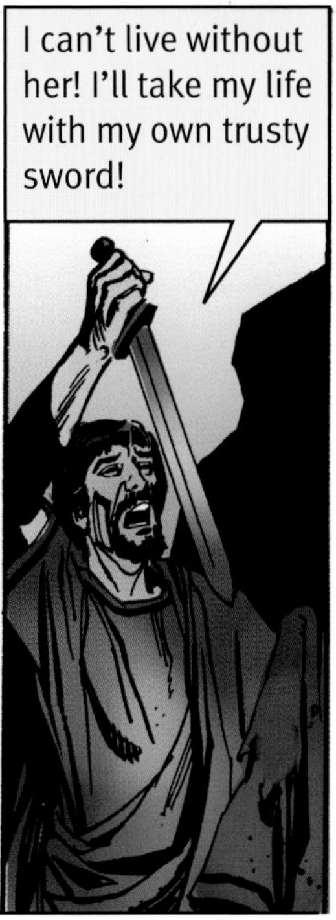
I can't live without her! I'll take my life with my own trusty sword!

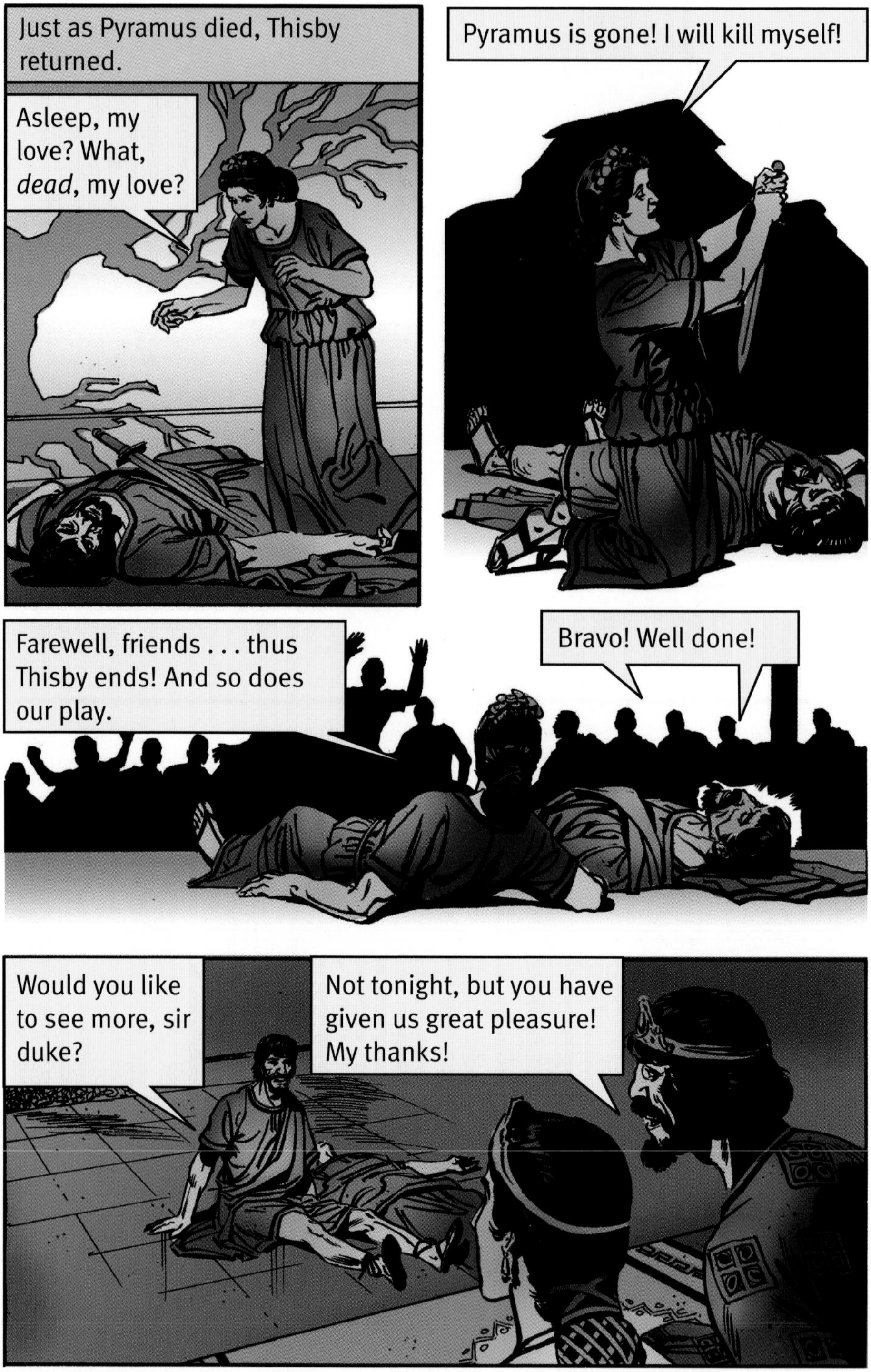
Just as Pyramus died, Thisby returned.
Asleep, my love? What, *dead*, my love?
Pyramus is gone! I will kill myself!
Farewell, friends . . . thus Thisby ends! And so does our play.
Bravo! Well done!
Would you like to see more, sir duke?
Not tonight, but you have given us great pleasure! My thanks!

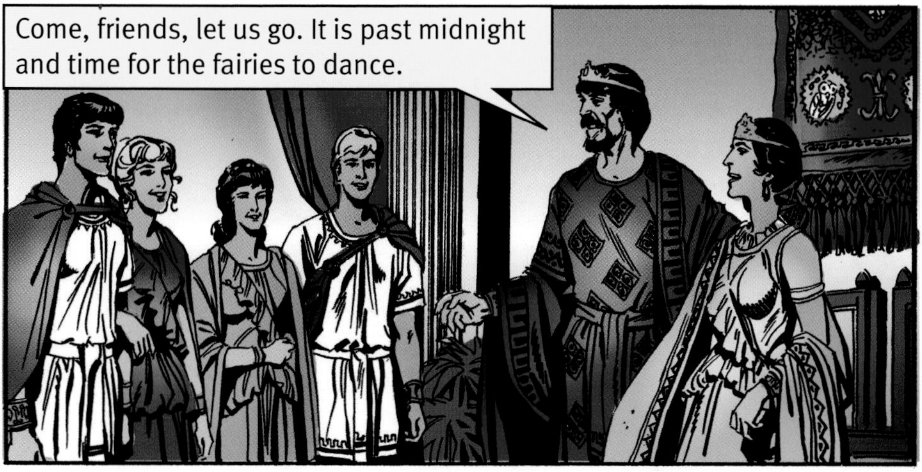
Come, friends, let us go. It is past midnight and time for the fairies to dance.

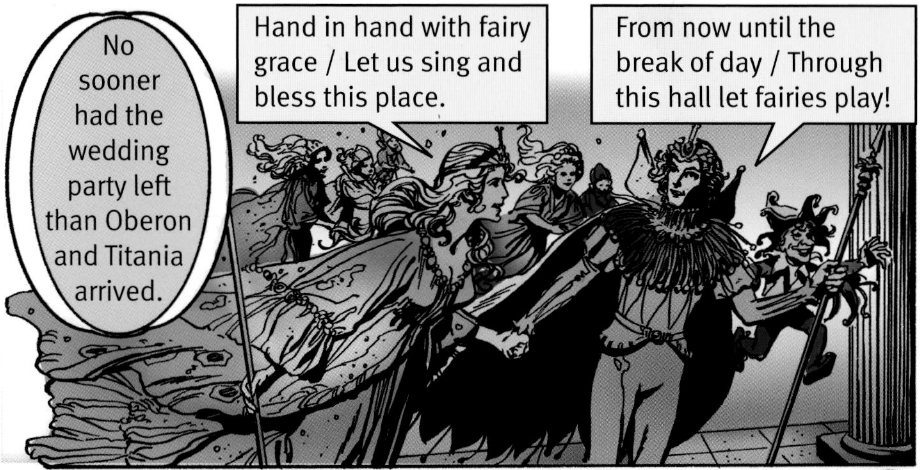
No sooner had the wedding party left than Oberon and Titania arrived.
Hand in hand with fairy grace / Let us sing and bless this place.
From now until the break of day / Through this hall let fairies play!

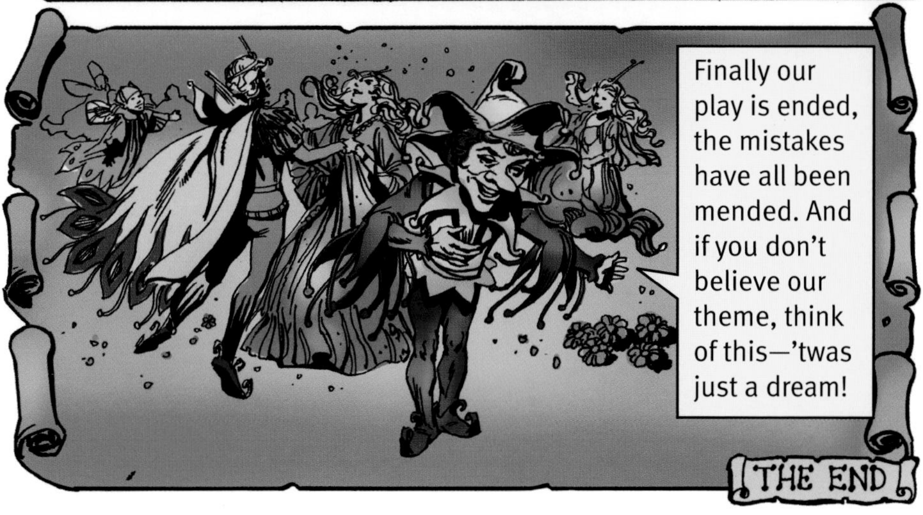
Finally our play is ended, the mistakes have all been mended. And if you don't believe our theme, think of this—'twas just a dream!
THE END